Countdown Madness

Zoey Zane

Cover Design:
Kristina Hack at Temys Designs Author
Logo Design:
Tanya Baikie at More Than Words Graphic Design
Editing and Formatting:
Rachelle Wright at R. A. Wright Editing
Proofreading:
Dee at Dee's Notes Proofreading and Editing Service

Dedication

To all the people who always wanted a romantic
scavenger hunt and never got one.

Me. It's me.

She lived for nights thick
with lust and romance and wine
and naked kisses.

Mason Fowler

Chapter One

Lizzy

STORMS ARE ONE OF the things I love most about Crimson, but what I love even more is what comes after the rain. Petrichor: the best smell in the whole world.

As I watch the mist that hugs the mountains, serenity washes over me. Many people fear storms, running away scared of what they bring. I run into a storm, begging it to calm my inner chaos until all is silent.

Standing up, I drape the blanket on the back of the bench and walk to the mailbox, realizing I never checked yesterday's mail. The mailbox is slightly ajar, leaving the corner of a large manila envelope peeking out. I open the mailbox, curious about what it is. A couple of bills and a magazine, but nothing else catches my attention.

As I slide the flap open, I peer into the envelope. There's a smaller envelope with something hard at the bottom. I turn it upside down and a key falls out. Turning over the key, I notice there's nothing on it. It's just a simple key. Reaching back into the manila envelope, I tug out a smaller envelope with the number ten written on it and rip it open. The note reads:

Here comes your next adventure. There will be a series of clues, beginning with this one. It will serve as your countdown to the day your big adventure begins. It is yours for the taking.

The next clue is where you went when things got tough at home. No friends, no neighbors, no family. Just you and your favorite thing.

"What the?" I mutter, confused. Turning the card over, there's no signature. I glance back at the envelope. There's no return address either. Just a postmark from the Crimson Post Office.

What the fuck? It's local, but who knows about my home life? I keep details of my childhood pretty tight-lipped when I can. However, there are some things I'd rather not talk about.

Puzzled, I walk back up to the porch and set the rest of the mail down on the table. I sit down on the couch and set the note on my lap. As I pick up my coffee and take a drink, I reread the postcard again and again, then switch between examining the big envelope and the small one. There's absolutely nothing on either one. No hints, no clues, nothing to tell me who sent this. After I finish the rest of my coffee, I make a decision. What's the worst that could happen?

The roads are wet, but there's not a lot of traffic this morning. My drive into town is short, and I don't have time to talk myself out of this. Before I know it, I'm parking my car in the lot by Crimson Credit Union. I take a deep breath and get out of the car. It's such a beautiful morning, and normally I'd enjoy it. But now, I rush into the bookstore, where Julie talks to Mr. Leon, the owner.

"Hello, Elizabeth!" Mr. Leon calls out.

I wave, not bothering to say hi back. I'm focused on one thing.

"Where is it?" I mutter, searching the shelves. It appears as though Mr. Leon has done some rearranging recently, making it more difficult to find the one I'm looking for.

When I was a young girl, I would spend countless hours in the children's section of the bookstore, reading every book I could get my hands on. My parents fought endlessly, right up until the moment my mother died. My mom worked at the credit union as a teller, back when it first opened. It was her first job, just like it was my first job. Because of my mom, I fell in love with numbers.

"There it is!"

I find my favorite book, ignoring that there is more than one copy. As I open it, a purple envelope falls out, and I chuckle. *Damn, I'm good.* Scooping up the paper, I see a nine written on it. I open the envelope, pull out the notecard, and see another clue.

Yay! You found me. You have officially begun the hunt for your true happiness. Here is the second clue.

I am made of red bricks where people see my friends fly. While many have suffered, the pretty colors fly high.

There's only one place where colors fly high in this town. Crimson Town Hall. Shaking my head, I walk back up to the front to chat with Julie.

I wave the notecard, and Julie raises her eyebrows.

"Hey, Lizzy. What's that?"

"You don't know?" She shakes her head. "I don't either." Laughing, I pull the first envelope out of my back pocket and hand it to her.

"A note?" she asks.

"Open it."

Julie hesitantly opens the envelope and pulls out the postcard. "Ten?"

"Turn it over."

She turns the card over in her hand and reads. Julie looks up at me, then looks back at the card. She reads it again. "And you're doing this?" she asks.

Silently, I hand her the second card.

Finally, Julie speaks. "I'm not sure what to make of it."

"That's what I'm thinking! Then I come here and find that. I mean, we live in a small town, so not many people would do something like this." My hands fly around—they move a lot when I talk. "Am I crazy?"

"I say, go for it! Who knows? Maybe Ethan has something up his sleeve?"

"I doubt it. He's not the type of guy to plan surprises." I huff and roll my eyes.

"Yeah, I can see that. He does have a stick up his ass, you know." She snorts, and a chuckle escapes me.

"Yeah, yeah."

"He's better once you get to know him," we say at the same time. Julie and Moxie always tease me about being with Ethan after so long. I have the itch for adventure—to experience the most I can out of life. Unfortunately, Ethan does not.

We've been engaged for six months, and while I hoped the engagement would ruffle his feathers or something, he acts disinterested, in a way. He's dragging his feet and wants to put things off for another year. It's difficult to plan a wedding when there's no date set.

Julie interrupts my wedding thoughts. "If it's not Ethan, do you know who it could be?"

"No idea." I shake my head. "I wouldn't even know where to begin!"

"Just be careful. Don't get tangled up in something you can't get out of. Crazies lurk everywhere."

"Yes, Mom." I laugh and walk toward the front of the store. "Well, I'm off to the town hall for the next clue. Call me later?"

"I'll be dying to know what happens!" she calls after me.

A sense of calm washes over me as I leave the bookstore. Julie is the level-headed one in my small group of friends, and while she's my age, she acts much older. Like me, we both have sick parents who require a great deal of care.

I'm hoping the clues are all in town. As long as they don't ask me to jump off a cliff or anything, I think I'll be fine. It is odd, though. Just in case, I pull out my phone and send Ethan a text.

Hi! Did you send me something in the mail?
A manila envelope with a key?

This is crazy! Call me before you head to work!

A few minutes later, on the outskirts of town, I arrive at the town hall. It was built in the early 1900s using only pure-red bricks. The American flag flies high in the air, secured to the pole standing to the right of the building. Behind the flag is Memorial Cemetery. Usually, I stop to admire the cemetery, see the flowers, and say a prayer for the ones we've lost—like my mom's brother, who died in Vietnam. But today, I can't stop.

Making my way into the building, I scan the area, searching for anything that would indicate where the clue is. Nothing stands out. I blindly turn a corner and smack right into Ernie, the security guard.

"Oof!"

"Oh my god, Ernie! I'm so sorry!" Ernie laughs, and I turn to make sure he's all right.

He waves me off and says, "I was wondering when you'd come in. I have something for you."

I give him a curious look and follow him down the hall to his desk. He sits down, opens the bottom drawer, and pulls out a blue envelope. "I believe this belongs to you."

"Where did this come from?" I ask. With a hand that's shaking—with excitement or uncertainty, I'm not sure—I take it from him. I turn over the envelope and see the number eight. "How long have you had this?"

"Don't be a buzzkill, Lizzy. You'll ruin the fun." He winks.

Groaning, I pull out the postcard. "Well, at least that confirms something bad isn't at the end of this."

Ernie laughs and slams a hand down on the counter. "Don't you worry, young lady. You'll be fine."

Glancing at the postcard, I realize it's the same handwriting as the purple and white ones. The handwriting doesn't seem familiar, but it's a beautiful cursive font, like an elegant calligraphy.

I am full of the wind. I am a butterfly. I'm where your first kiss happened. Where am I?

My first kiss . . . a butterfly . . . oh my god, the school! "Thank you, Ernie!" I lean over the counter and kiss his cheek.

"Good luck!" He smiles with a twinkle in his eye.

Okay, this has got to be Ethan. We were talking about first kisses and first loves just the other day. What's he doing? We're already engaged. Did he get promoted? No. It's not my birthday, and it's not my mom's either. It's not our anniversary. What is this?! Oh man, I'm kind of excited!

Crimson has been home for my entire twenty-six years on this earth. There's only one place I can think of with butterflies—the football field of the primary school. We only have two schools in Crimson—Butterflies: the years K-8 primary school, and Cardinals: the years 9-12 secondary school.

When I pull up to the Butterflies school, memories of my first kiss come rushing back. It was right before school let out for the summer, just after my fifteenth birthday. Tucker, my best friend, was my first kiss. I had been complaining that I didn't want to start high school without having been kissed. My father was sending me to a summer camp to get me out of his hair, and I remember rambling on and on about being the last to experience anything and how much I didn't want to die a virgin, even though a simple kiss wasn't the same thing as my virginity. Extreme for a fifteen-year-old, yes, but everything feels life-altering at that age. Maybe to shut me up, or maybe to help, I'm not sure, but Tucker grabs my waist and pulls me in for a panty-melting kiss. I had read about it in books and heard friends talk about it, but never experienced it until Tucker.

Most first kisses are messy, sloppy, and useless. But not mine. Mine was an earth-shattering, stuck-in-your-brain kiss—one you'll relive every time you kiss someone else. Until that day, I never saw Tucker as anything other than my best friend. For better or worse, he changed my life. I've had other kisses since then, and I'm not going to die a virgin, but there was never a match for Tucker's kiss. Nothing measures up to that high bar that I'm sure I'll never reach again.

Lost in thought, I wander around the field until I reach the bleachers. Taped to the handrail of the stairs, I see a pink envelope. Once again, a beautiful script greets me.

Memories can be manipulated over time, but this one you'll never lose. From age three to ninety-nine, I'll always stay. Come find me.

Riddles have never been my thing, but this one didn't even take me a second. It's referring to my childhood home, where I first learned of my parents' divorce.

Looking back, I can easily see how they came to the conclusion that they needed to separate. Sure, it was devastating, especially for an eight-year-old. But it was time for them. Jogging back to my car, my heart hurts a little, knowing where I'm heading next.

It's easy to say now they should have gotten divorced sooner. It's easy to think about two Christmases, two birthdays, two of everything. What's not easy is knowing it never happened due to unforeseen circumstances. It's not easy watching my father drown his sorrows in a bottle because he picked a fight with my mom the day she died in a car accident caused by a ruptured brain aneurysm on her birthday. It's not easy being a little girl and trying to pick up the pieces. And it definitely wasn't easy being on my own on that day, and on the anniversary of that day, even years later.

I've only been back to my childhood home twice since he sold it all those years ago. We stayed in it for a couple of years after Mom died, but it was too hard to keep living there. Father started drinking, lost his job, and got behind on the bills. He sold our house to pay them, and we moved into a tiny apartment across town. That's where I met Tucker. He was my next-door neighbor.

We finished growing up together and have been inseparable ever since. Amy—Tucker's mom—helped take care of me when my father couldn't. I spent many nights on their couch to avoid my father's drunken rage. She also taught me all the girly things you learn from your mom. She could never replace my mom, but it helped to have someone close to talk to. Amy and Tucker became my second family.

That's why my first kiss took me by such surprise. It never occurred to me that I could be in love with Tucker.

I didn't swoon over him the way other girls did. He was my best friend, who knew all my secrets, and I knew all of his. Until that fiery moment, I had only *thought* I knew what lust was. Tucker lit me up in all the right places, places I didn't know existed. Cliché, I know, but that kiss changed my life forever.

Pulling up to the house, I notice the owners haven't been taking care of the place. *Does anyone even live here anymore?* Plants are overgrown and are attempting to take over the porch. Tears fill my eyes, and I blink furiously to stop them from falling. I sit in my car for a few minutes before getting out and walking to the mailbox. There's a huge stack of mail, like the owners didn't leave a forwarding address. Sitting right on top is a green envelope with the number six written on it. I quickly tear it open:

Beyond the score of your childhood, beyond the scope of your reality, you've always dreamed of leaving. Find me where you've always wanted to go.

This one is tough. Sighing, I walk back to my car, noticing it's much later than I realized. It's time to call it a night.

Driving in the direction of home, my stomach growls. Amy—my surrogate mom—still loves to keep me fed.

I've got a huge bowl of homemade mac and cheese waiting for me when I get home.

The drive home doesn't take as long as it normally does. After pulling into the driveway, I climb out of the car and walk up to the front porch, where I left the rest of the mail, my morning coffee, and the blanket. I pick everything up, unlock the door, and walk inside.

While I wait for my dinner to heat up, I start my nightly 15-minute clutter purge. It's silly to Tucker—he thinks I should live in a "lived-in" house. I argue that my place *is* lived in, but I like it to be picked up. All the things lying on the floor and the counters drive me crazy.

Tucker gives me the most shit for it when he comes over. He'll deliberately leave the pillow on the windowsill instead of putting it back on the couch because he knows it drives me up the wall. I chuckle at the thought of throwing the pillow at him.

The timer dings to let me know dinner is ready. I grab the bowl out of the oven, pick up my soda, and settle on the couch. I glance at my phone. I'm dying to call Ethan to tell him what's going on, but he hates it when I interrupt his business dinners. There are no texts or missed calls from him. Before I can second-guess myself, I decide to send him some quick texts.

You didn't text me before work as you always do. Hope everything is ok.

I have exciting news! I'm moving further along in the hunt – this is so fun! What have you gotten me into?

Can't wait to see you, call me soon so we can talk! Love you, babe.

I place the phone back on the coffee table and put my feet up as I press play. *Definitely, Maybe* with Ryan Reynolds lights up the living room in the otherwise dark house.

It's been an emotional day. A feel-good movie, feel-good food, and being cuddled up in the softest blanket known to man is exactly what I need right now.

Chapter Two

Lizzy

"Oww!" I CRY OUT, my body desperately in need of a good stretch as I shift my position on the couch. I can't believe I didn't get up last night. As I twist my limbs into comfortable positions and my muscles relax, a sense of relief flows through me. My breathing has slowed, and the raindrops outside seem louder, like the sound is coming from inside my house.

My phone vibrates against the coffee table. Tucker's face greets me, and I slide my finger across the screen to answer.

"It's so early," I groan.

"Well, good morning, Sunshine!" He chuckles. "What are your plans today?"

"Actually . . ." I pause. I really wanted to tell Ethan first, but he never texted me back last night. "I'm on a scavenger hunt."

"Oh, really?"

"It's really weird, though—"

"What? What do you mean?"

"Okay, so, I checked the mail yesterday—I didn't check it the day before, so I'm not sure how long it's been sitting in the mailbox—but there was a manila envelope with another envelope inside it labeled with the number ten and a key. I have no idea what the key is or where it leads to, but I'm hoping these clues will tell me."

"A key? Clues?" He doesn't like it when I talk a mile a minute.

"Yes, Tucker, keep up!" Laughing, I continue. "The first clue led me to the bookstore, where I found the second clue. That one lead me to the town hall. Then, the next clue took me to Butterflies. And I'm not done."

"You're not?" His laugh is music to my ears. "How surprising."

Sitting up on the couch, I gaze out the window to admire the view. The mountains are covered in darkness, rain cascades down in waves, and nothing is better than the scene before me. The appearance of beauty comes from the soul. Not many people enjoy the rain or storms in general, but me? I'm here for it all.

I take a breath and continue. "Nope. That last clue actually took me to the bleachers where you kissed me." My heart flutters when I hear his sharp intake of breath, but it shouldn't. I'm with Ethan, and Tucker and I aren't a thing. We can't be. We'll never be. I can't imagine my life without Tucker: my best friend, my favorite person.

"Next, the clue from the bleachers led me home. Well, to my parents' home. From before. And oh, shit. I forgot to tell you! Whoever owns it now is not taking care of it. There were overgrown plants, and honestly, it just looks trashy. I'm a little hurt by it, which I know is ridiculous, but I can't help it. That's where I remember my mom the most, you know?"

"Oh, Lizzy. That's not ridiculous," he says sadly.

"It is, but okay." I roll my eyes. "Their mailbox was almost overflowing with mail. Like, who doesn't leave a forwarding address? Is that something you can check on for me? Who sold it and just left it? Please, Tucker?" I don't bother to let him reply before moving on. "So, on top of that huge stack was another frigging envelope. I open it up and it says something about a place I've always dreamt of going to. That's where the next clue will be. The only thing I can think of is Italy, but there's no way I can fly across the world at a moment's notice just for a damn clue."

He's laughing again. "Lizzy."

"What?" A chuckle leaves my mouth too.

"Slow down, Sunshine. No, you're not traveling across the world for a clue. That could be dangerous. Was there a name on the clues? Do you even know where they're coming from?"

"Wait. You don't know?" I ask seriously. "It's Ethan! Come on, it's gotta be!"

Silence.

"Tucker, you there?"

He clears his throat. "I'm here."

"Good. Anyway, this last one has me stumped. I came home after that last clue and have been thinking about it all night, snuggled up with a good blanket, food, and a movie just to clear my head. I mean, come on. We know if I fixate on it, I'll never figure it out—I have to take a breather. So now you're all caught up. What do you think?"

"I think you need to be careful," he says.

"What do you think is going to happen? It's Ethan!"

He sighs. "You know how I feel about him."

"Come with me! It'll be fun."

"Just be careful is all I'm saying."

"Yes, sir."

Tucker lets out a small groan. "Lizzy."

"What?"

"Uh—nothing. It's okay."

"Just be happy for me. Ethan will be at the end of this with a thousand yellow daisies and candles, and it'll be amazing."

Silence.

"I need to go," Tucker says. "We'll talk later, okay?"

"Wait, Tuck—" The line goes dead.

What's his problem? I shake off the negative thoughts. *Today will be a good day, I just know it.*

Italy. Italy. Italy. It keeps repeating over and over again in my mind as I go through the day. I'm preoccupied at work with spreadsheet after spreadsheet after spreadsheet. Spreadsheets are one of my happy places, but I still can't concentrate. People can murky the waters, but numbers are the calm within the storm. When the ledger or balance sheet aligns and each side matches, its pluses and minuses the same, the chaos of the world slips away.

A million thoughts run through my head as each hour passes, and I'm becoming more frustrated. I push away the keyboard and turn off the monitors. After quickly grabbing my things, I head into Melanie's office.

I peek my head in. "Hey, I'm heading out early today. Gotta run some errands," I say. I've only been here for a couple of hours.

Without glancing up from her notebook, she says, "Great, have a good night!"

The rain has let up a little as I make my way to my car. It's a small drizzle now compared to the downpour it was this morning. I start the car and drive toward home, but partway there, I slam on the brakes.

Wait! If I can't go to Italy, I'll make Italy come to me. It's the only option! I make a U-turn. There's only one Italian restaurant in town. They make the best lasagna, almost as if they import it straight from Italy.

It's not too busy when I pull into the parking lot. I head inside and greet the owner, Milo, an older gentleman.

He smiles and asks, "The usual, to go?"

My stomach grumbles in response. "Yes, please. I guess I forgot to eat breakfast today."

"Be out in ten!" he says.

Glancing around me, I take in my surroundings. The only thing that looks different is the bulletin board. There's a huge map of Italy with an orange envelope pinned to Venice, the number five in that familiar, curly script on the front. I walk over to it and pull the pin out. *It has to be for me.* Putting the pin back in its place, I slide the envelope into my back pocket and take a seat.

Milo comes around the corner soon after, bringing a delicious smell with him. "I put some extra rolls in there for you."

"Oh, thank you! You're so good to me, Milo!" I slide him a twenty-dollar bill. "Keep the change."

As soon as I make it safely back into my car, I set the lasagna on the passenger seat and open the envelope.

Skipped rocks fall to their death, which is where I am. Can you find me?

A scoff escapes my lips. "Falling to their death? What?" *Oh my god. Ethan is crazy.* This riddle is too easy—there's only one place where you can skip rocks in Crimson. The lake. It's also a great place to eat lunch. There's a covered picnic area to shield me from the rain.

It was one of my favorite places to go in high school. I've spent many summers and fall nights there, enjoying the weather, cuddling up to the bonfire when it got colder, and roasting marshmallows with friends.

The lake is where I learned to swim, to steer a boat, and to water ski. So much laughter and good memories come flooding back during the drive there.

The parking lot is deserted when I arrive. Not even the boaters are out today, not that I blame them. I think I'm one of the only ones that actually crave the rain and everything that comes with it. When I come upon the picnic tables, I spot a black envelope taped to a pole. *Number four.* Shaking my head, I can't help myself. I tear it open to find the next clue.

Almost there. While I am here, they are all there. The place where couples go.

Ha, that's easy too! Make-out Point! My younger self did spend many nights there. Every town had one, even small ones like Crimson.

Excitement courses through my body. My stomach grumbles again, reminding me I haven't eaten yet. I sit down on the bench and eat. *It's so good.* Milo definitely knows how to make the best, most authentic lasagna. He is from Italy, after all.

The rain echoes off the tin roof. I could listen to that sound all day. Within a few minutes, I eat everything Milo made. The extra rolls were just what I needed to finish off the meal. I toss my garbage into the trash can and jog back to the car to keep myself from getting too wet.

I'm almost home with the clue from Make-out Point when it occurs to me. I still haven't heard from Ethan today. No texts, no calls, nothing. Which is odd, considering he usually texts me throughout the day. I've been caught up in the hunt, and I didn't realize I hadn't heard from him.

Instead of turning down the road to go home, I turn in the opposite direction and head over to his apartment.

His car is in the parking lot when I arrive, and I park in a visitor's space. *Wait, isn't he supposed to be at a business dinner?*

I fish his key out of my handbag and walk toward the door. Unlocking the door, I let myself into the living room. Immediately, I notice something is off—there's a shift in the air. Then I stumble, tripping over something.

"What the?" I mumble as I bend down to pick it up. Ethan keeps his place tidy. There shouldn't be anything on the floor. I hold up the item, and my whole body shudders in disgust as I realize it's a black lace bra. This is a shocking revelation. Not that this is a black lace bra, but the fact that it's not mine. The cups are too small to be mine. Someone else's black lace bra is on the floor of my fiancé's apartment.

His bedroom door opens, and out comes a woman. She turns on the lamp next to the coffee table, illuminating her appearance.

"Wait . . . Kristie?" I take a step forward.

She turns to face me. "Oh shit."

My hand goes up to silence her. I walk past her, storming into the bedroom. The brown eyes I always adored stare up at me—he's a deer caught in the headlights.

Without giving him a chance to speak, I go first.

"Ethan . . . what the fuck have you done to us?"

Chapter Three

Lizzy

A BLAST OF THUNDER shakes me to my core as a streak of lightning lights up my bedroom. I haven't been able to sleep. Not a wink all night, just tossing and turning. *How fucking dare he?* The image of his eyes looking up at me, almost as if he never expected to get caught, burrows into my mind.

I guess all the signs were there. He barely texted me anymore, hid his phone in my presence, and always found an excuse to leave or to not invite me to his place. I mean, we were getting married, for god's sake! It can't be that hard to keep his dick in his pants. *Fuck!* And those business dinners? I bet he was with her. *Goddamn Kristie. Goddamn Ethan.*

I groan in frustration and roll onto my side.

My phone dings a few times back-to-back. I reach for it on the nightstand and unlock it. There are nine texts, all from Ethan.

Baby. It isn't what it looks like.

Come on, she doesn't mean anything.

You're the only one for me.

I didn't mean for it to happen.

She just needed a place to stay for a few nights.

I would never hurt you.

It was only one time, I'll never do it again.

Please don't leave me.

I love you.

No. I can't do this. After silencing the ringer, I set the phone facedown on the nightstand and let out another scream of frustration. *Okay, get a grip. I can't lay in bed all day. Wallowing never did anyone any good.*

I gaze around the room, stopping at the latest clue sitting on my dresser. Taunting me. Mocking me. If it wasn't Ethan hiding the clues all over town, who was it? The further the numbers count down, the more intrigued I become with the madness. My mind continues to run a hundred miles an hour, still with no answer. All bets are off with Ethan now. That's it. We're over. He wouldn't plan an extravagant scavenger hunt if he was cheating, right? It's not possible. Besides, he's never been the romantic type. Is this thing considered romantic? Ugh. I don't even know what this is anymore.

The latest clue keeps calling to me—the red envelope with the number three on it that was taped to the sign of Crimson Mountain Hills.

The more I think about it, the more I realize each of these clues means something important or indicates a significant change in my life. The bookstore, town hall, Butterflies, my childhood home. All of those events happened before high school. Then Italy, the lake, Make-out Point. Those are all things I experienced in high school and beyond. And yet, none of this information tells me what I want to know now.

Picking up the envelope, I flip it over and over in my hand. I've got two choices: I can wallow in self-pity all day, which isn't going to help, or I can finish what I started and get out of bed. I sigh and open the envelope.

You will get hungry when you see me. I am always fresh, and my plumpness is a treat!

How can I even think about food right now? I glare at the ceiling, and my head hits the pillow again. Cookies always make me hungry, but they're not plump. Mmm, double-fudge brownies too. Those are my favorite in the whole world. *Wait a second.* It's Saturday, and that means one thing in Crimson: the farmers' market.

I don't think I've ever gotten out of bed so quickly. I love the farmers' market. Everything is so fresh, and I swear I devour half the fruit in my basket before I even make it home. I can't help it!

It doesn't take me long to get ready, pulling my unbrushed hair into a ponytail and going without makeup. I make it to the market in record time, and I stop to take in everything around me. Thankfully, the rain has stopped for now. The day is not quite sunny, but still glorious. The air is crisp, and a gentle breeze floats around me. People are walking around, in no hurry and with nowhere to go, shuffling in and out of the booths.

The farmers' market is quite the spectacle around Crimson. Visitors from all over the state and neighboring states come to enjoy its various treats. Dozens of vendors line the perimeter, each one different from the next. You never know what you'll find here—that's part of the appeal.

Dodging shoulders and careful not to step on anyone's toes, I make my way to the fruit section. Before long, the basket is brimming with fruits. Apples, oranges, peaches; even some vegetables made it into the basket. Each booth has something for me, but there's still no clue. Just as I'm about to leave, I realize I forgot the strawberries—my favorite. Weaving in and out of the crowd, I finally stumble upon the plump strawberries. Red, delicious, and tempting. I'm compelled to grab four containers and make my way to the register. Claire greets me and rings up the strawberries.

"It's so nice to see you today, Lizzy. How's your day going?"

Claire is rather new in town, but she's quickly become one of my favorite vendors. She's super sweet, and she pours everything she has into these strawberries.

"I'm having a weird week," I say. She reaches for the cash in my hand. I shake my head. "So, Ethan and I are over. It's fine," I say before she says anything sympathetic. "Then I'm being sent all over town for a scavenger hunt. I don't even know who's leading it, but I'm having fun, or I was, until Ethan. All these old memories are coming up, and it's just a lot. It's been a weird week."

Woah. Saying it out loud gives it more finality than I thought it would.

"Sounds like it. I'm sorry to hear about Ethan." She gives me a small smile and hands me a receipt.

"Thank you. Have a great day, Claire. See you around."

"You too. Take care."

I toss the receipt in my basket and stop for a minute. There's a gold envelope between the receipt and my change. *Wait, what's this?* I turn around and hold up the envelope in question.

"Just go with it." She winks and moves to the next customer.

After a brisk stroll back to my car, I tear open the gold envelope with the number two on the front. It reads:

The key you hold is the key to your happiness. You shall find it at Number 215.

I fumble in my purse, pull the white envelope out, and locate the key. I flip it over in my fingers but find nothing written on the back. It's not a key to any house in town, as far as I can tell. It's too big. Maybe it's for a lock of some kind, or maybe the key to a safe? It's too big for a car or a motorcycle.

The town's buildings pass by as I drive back home. The library. The school. The fire station. The plaza.

None of those places will have a slot to fit this key. I glance at the key sitting on the passenger seat. It's taunting me. Crimson Police Department is on my left, and the Crimson Post Office is on my right.

"Ahh!" A lightbulb turns on in my head. The post office has a couple of bigger boxes that have larger keys. It's got to be a perfect fit.

I make my way into the building, noting the front counter is closed. The post office boxes are around the corner behind the package drop-off.

I wave to a few people as I walk down the hall lined with boxes. Numbers 500 - 450 are on my right. Numbers 450 - 400 are on the left. Each section contains fifty mailboxes, and as I continue walking down the row, the numbers get lower. Dragging my finger along the wall like it's a chain-link fence, I finally find number 215. As I slowly slide the key in and turn it, I let out a gasp. It actually opens.

In the box is another manila envelope. Sweat beads my forehead, and my hands tremble as I reach into the box. The first thing I see is the words *open me*. I dump the contents onto the counter behind me. There are two teal envelopes, the same size as the others. I open the one with the number one on it.

You've almost reached the end. Congratulations! In this envelope, there is a clue, a letter, and another key. Once you arrive at 526 Sandbury Road, open the letter and read it. Do not read it before you get there. Promise me.

Promise me? This address sounds familiar. I flip over the card to see what's on the other side. Nothing. The second envelope must contain the letter and the key. I pocket all the contents and head back to my car.

My phone rings, and it cuts me off mid-thought. Ethan's ugly face appears in the middle of the car's console. I immediately poke my finger at the decline button.

No. He doesn't get to call me.

The phone rings again. I decline the call again.

It rings for the third time. As I debate answering the call, my finger develops a mind of its own and pushes the accept button.

When my brain catches up, I hang up before he can say anything. There's nothing he could say that would make this remotely okay.

It rings again. I scream at the console as I answer.

"Leave me the fuck alone," I yell and hang up again.

The phone rings a fifth time. Decline.

It rings once more. *That's it!* I press accept.

"Ethan, we're over. I don't want to hear it." I hang up again.

I can't deal with this shit right now. I scroll through the contacts on my phone until I find him and block his number. A flood of relief washes over me. I don't think I've ever used the block button on my phone before, and it feels good. Sure, I've blocked people on social media, but never with calls. There's a first time for everything.

I refuse to be one of those girls. You know the ones—the ones who break down into tears every time their boyfriend does something wrong. The ones who beat themselves down because he cheated or he wasn't paying attention to them. The pitiful ones. I've never been that girl, and I never will be. Yes, it hurts, but there's nothing I can do about that now. My mom wasn't here when I got my first boyfriend or my first breakup, or really any of my firsts. My father is the one who tucks any sign of emotion away to deal with later. I've learned from the best.

While my phone is still open, I google the address on the card. 526 Sandbury Road. Ah, that's why it sounds familiar. It's a huge country house on the outskirts of the opposite side of town. Crimson is a small town, but unless you're traveling through, you don't go out to the edges often. It's easy to stay in a small circle and not venture farther out.

I remember admiring this house when I was younger. It was much bigger than my childhood home. I remember wanting to fill it with children, loud children who would grow up to be artists or musicians, police officers, or whoever they wanted to be. Then those children would have children, and my mom would still be alive for her grandchildren and great-grandchildren. Tears spring to my eyes as I remember my mom won't be here for any of that.

Wiping away a fallen tear, I take a shaky breath and steady myself. *I can do this*. I put my car in drive and pop on some music.

The automated voice comes from the speaker, interrupting the song. "You have arrived at your destination."

It startles me, and I glance around outside the car. There's an unrecognizable car on the right side of the house, next to the wall of trees obscuring the view from the road. Overgrown brush swallows the walkway to the side, and the front porch railing is falling off. There's a stair missing on the porch, and the front door is slightly ajar.

Whoever owns this house let it become neglected. The windows are shattered, and the shutters are crooked. The once vibrant gray exterior is now yellowing and peeling in patches.

Still, I've always loved this house. My curiosity wins once again, and I grab the manila envelope before getting out of the car. I lean against the driver's side door of my Jeep, open the second teal envelope, and pull out an old letter. I gasp as I unfold it. This time, I do recognize the handwriting.

Oh, my darling Lizzy. Thank you for taking such a huge leap of faith to get here. You have no idea how worried I was. You grew up a little scared, to say the least, and I was afraid you wouldn't grow out of it. It means so much to me to know you're standing there reading this letter. I am so sorry I'm not here to see your smiling face. I'm so proud of you. Here you are, beyond twenty-five years, and I'm sure you are still as amazing as you ever were.

I wish I could see you now! I'll miss you so much. You're currently riding your bike up and down the street as I write this, and I am cherishing this moment so much it hurts. I'm sorry to leave you so young. It's almost my time, but I know I will see you again soon, after you've lived a long and happy life.

By the time you read this, I'm assuming you have an amazing boyfriend or husband. If not, you cannot have this present, and your father was a bonehead for giving this to you. It was the one thing we could actually agree on, for once. Go figure. I hope you enjoy this gift with all your heart, and I hope you find true happiness.

Go start your new adventure with your loved ones, here, in your new house. And maybe have a couple of grandkids for me? I'm watching over you, always.

I love you to the moon and beyond.

Mom

The tears flow, and I wipe my eyes on my sleeve. My new house. *My new house.* I can't believe what's in front of me.

I walk up the driveway just as my best friend walks out the front door, stopping me dead in my tracks. "Tucker? What are you doing here?"

Chapter Four

HIS GRIN IS SO big, it reaches his ears. "I'm here to welcome you home." He gestures toward the house.

"It's mine?" I hold up the letter from my mom. "And this? Where'd you get this? What is all this? Wait, are *you* behind the scavenger hunt? Tucker Banks!"

Tucker chuckles and puts his hand up to stop me. "Woah, so many questions! Be patient."

"I don't have patience, you know this." I stand with my hand on my hip. "Start 'splainin'."

He rolls his eyes. "Yes, that's a letter from your mom. Yes, this is your new house. Want a tour?"

"Yes!" I jump up and down, eliciting a belly laugh from Tucker.

We walk up the sidewalk, and when we come to the steps, he goes first. He holds his hand out for me to grab. "Be careful—the steps are weak."

I take his hand and steady myself. His hand is so warm, and my fingers tingle as they easily entwine with his. Why does this feel so right? A shiver rips through me.

Tucker leads me into the musky house. While it's overcast outside, there's plenty of natural light as we walk down the hallway into a living room. In contrast to the exterior, the interior of the house isn't too bad.

It needs a fresh coat of paint, among other things, but it looks like someone has been through and cleaned it recently. It's not as dusty as I thought it would be.

"The kitchen is to the left, through the dining room. Take a peek at the fireplace."

He steps to the side and reveals a fireplace with a rather large couch in front of it. The fireplace is clean, with a neat stack of wood inside, urging me to light it. This place could use some warmth. On the couch are a couple of blankets and pillows.

"Oh my." I gasp as I take it in. Sitting in front of the fireplace with a cozy blanket, a cup of apple cider, and a book in my hand is one of my favorite things in the world. "I love it!"

Tucker walks down the hallway leading to the kitchen, pulling me behind him. I squeeze his hand, and he stops and glances back at me.

"Are you okay?"

"I'm—" I take a breath. "I'm not sure. I have so many questions, and you're not answering them. And then there's this thing with Ethan . . . who cheated on me, by the way. It's a mess. Then there's this. I don't know what we're doing, what's going on, and—" My voice cracks. I can't stop it. My eyes well, and tears fall down my cheeks.

"Oh, Lizzy." He spins around to face me, reaching up to wipe away a falling tear. As he inches closer to me, backing me up against the wall, I feel the warmth of his body against mine, the fire seeping from his soul.

I close my eyes and hang my head slightly. "I'm not good enough for him. The two years we spent together weren't enough for him. I wasn't enough . . ."

Tucker lifts my chin. "If you were mine, I'd push you against the wall and kiss the hell out of you. You are *more* than enough. If he doesn't think so, screw him. He's not worth it."

His words spark something inside me. It takes me back to our first kiss, and the butterflies in my stomach come to life. My breath quickens, and I can't think of anything else but him. Tucker. My best friend.

He tucks a piece of fallen hair behind my ear, caressing my cheek with his thumb as he does. "Now here's what we're going to do. You're going to take a minute to cry if you need to. Cry the hardest you can and get it all out because when you're done, that's it. We're not crying over him ever again. Then you're going to pick your chin up and see the rest of this property."

I sniffle and then nod. "Yes, okay."

"Yes, what?"

I know what he wants, and I can't resist taking the opportunity to bait him. "Yes, sir."

Tucker stifles a groan. "Go." He backs up and lets me take a few steps to the right.

Keeping my back to him, I let a few tears slip down my cheeks. I take a deep breath, wipe the tears away, and put a small smile on my face. Tucker's right.

Ethan's not worth crying over any longer. I need to move on. When I turn around to face him, there's a dark look on his face. One eyebrow is arched, and his almond-brown eyes swirl with caramel flecks. I'd almost say he looks . . . heated. There's something sinfully dark about him.

"I'm ready."

"Let's go." He holds out his hand, gesturing down the hallway. "After you."

We venture into the kitchen where it's just as clean as the area by the fireplace.

"Come on, Tucker. What is this?" I slowly spin around, taking everything in.

"It's your new kitchen." He smirks as he walks to the freezer and opens it to reveal a bottle of whiskey. I laugh.

"Oh, you came prepared?"

"Can't celebrate your new house without something to drink." He takes the bottle out and sets it on the counter. "Why don't you look around some more while I call and order pizza?"

"Pepperoni, please!"

"Would I get anything different? Silly girl." He laughs as I walk out of the kitchen and into another hallway leading to the bedrooms.

The bedrooms are bigger than what I thought they would be. A small pang hits my chest as I wander through the house. My mom left me this house—the house I admired as a kid. How did I not know we owned it? How did she know I wanted it? There are still so many questions and no answers.

Tucker knows more than he's letting on.

I trail into what used to be the library. It's a decent-sized room too, with built-in bookshelves and a reading nook off in the corner. Oh, the possibilities for a room like this! The excitement spreads through me, and I want to celebrate, even if I no longer have a fiancé.

As I wander through the house back into the kitchen, where Tucker is scrolling through his phone, I can't help but feel a shift in the wind.

He peers up when he hears me walk into the room. "Pizza will be here any minute."

"Sounds good. I'm hungrier than I thought."

He turns to face me. "So, what do you think?"

"I think I have a million questions, and I need some answers."

He glances at the clock on his phone. "Okay. You have until the pizza gets here. Go."

"Why do you have a letter from my mom?"

"My mom gave it to me."

"Amy did? Why?"

He shrugs. "I guess your dad gave it to her."

"What about this house? Where'd it come from?"

"I've viewed the property records and the original deed. It was foreclosed on, and your mom bought it at auction for a steal. Why, I don't know. All I know is it's your name on the deed now. She signed it over to you before she passed. It's your house."

"Wow." I sigh. Before I can ask another question, there's a knock on the door.

"Time's up!" Tucker smiles and rushes to the door for the pizza.

As I turn to look around the room again, I'm trying to wrap my head around what he told me. I can't believe my mom gave me a house. It's the last thing I have of her. Sure, I have some photographs, but nothing to give me a sense of home. She pictured me in this house, married, with kids and eventually grandkids.

Tucker calls my name from the other room, snapping me out of my thoughts.

"Coming!" I yell. I swipe the bottle of whiskey from the counter and walk into the living room. He's hunched over, lighting the wood for a fire. The two pillows are on either end of the couch, waiting for us, with the pizza box in the middle.

"I thought we could eat here. Start a fire, drink, and think."

"Sounds perfect." I plop down onto the couch and open the pizza box, grab a slice, and take a bite. "Oh man, this is so good. Milo makes the best pizza."

Tucker nods in agreement as he grabs a slice and sits down facing me.

"Oh, that reminds me, this scavenger hunt," I ask between bites. "I know you're a part of it, but who's the conductor? I found one of the clues at Milo's."

Tucker raises an eyebrow.

"I thought you said it was Ethan?" he says.

"I mean, yeah, I thought so. But why would he do all this if he was cheating? Wait a freaking second. How did you know I'd be here?"

He picks up the whiskey bottle and takes a big gulp, then coughs. "Ahh, that burns. I forgot how much I don't like whiskey."

I laugh. "True. You're more of a Jose kind of guy. You also didn't answer my question." I reach for the bottle and take a swig. Whiskey is my go-to drink. It's gotten me through many events, both good and bad. My mom loved whiskey, too, and so did my father, apparently.

"I'm not sure how to answer it." He takes a bite and chews. After he swallows, he says, "I did warn you about Ethan. I didn't like him, and I still don't. He's an asshole."

"He cheated on me with Kristie." I frown. Kristie is also a real estate agent and works with Tucker in the same office.

"It doesn't surprise me. Bitch'll fuck anything with a dick." Tucker takes the bottle from me and takes another swig. "Ugh, this is gross."

"More for me then." I snatch it back and angrily take a sip.

We make small talk, and he tells me about Moxie's fight to get more money for the expansion of the club his mom owns. Moxie is the manager of The Twilight Club, the only strip club in Crimson. They're looking to expand it by adding a restaurant at the end of the building.

It's getting dark by the time we finish the pizza. I'm about five shots in, and Tucker isn't that far behind me. We're laughing and having a good time when Tucker pulls out his phone and turns on some music.

He puts the playlist on shuffle, and the first song that comes on—a love song—has tears gathering in my eyes. Blinking furiously doesn't stop them. He grabs my hand and pulls me closer to him. "Come here. I thought we weren't going to cry anymore." He wraps his arm around my shoulder, holding me tight.

"I know, but it sucks. I pictured a life with him. Hell, I was going to marry him. It was easy, comfortable, even. I wanted my sunshine and rainbows. But it wasn't for me. I guess I wasn't good enough."

Tucker hugs me closer. "No, Lizzy. He wasn't enough for you. You'd never be his sunshine, not the way you want. You're the lightning to my thunder, the beauty to my despair. You're the answer to my question and the calm to my chaos."

Tilting my head, I look up at him through tear-stained lashes. "Thank you."

"Hush. I'm going to kiss you until all you remember is the taste of me."

Maybe it's the alcohol talking. Maybe it's the truth. Either way, it sounds so damn good. Before I can finish nodding, his lips capture mine. My lips part, granting him access. He tastes like sin-covered whiskey, and I'll be damned if it isn't the best thing I've ever had on my tongue.

I need more.

I jump up and wrap my legs around him, and he cradles my ass while he devours my mouth. The kiss is hot and electric. Wrapped in each other, he lowers us down onto the couch, where we were moments before.

Chapter Five

Tucker

SHE'S A CRAVING THAT will never be satisfied. I never once imagined I'd fall for my best friend. Not until our first kiss. It was ages ago, but I knew then, at that moment, she was mine.

She moans into my lips, encouraging me. Her hand grabs my shirt, pulls me closer.

Our tongues meld together, and we're running out of breath. I guide her head back and hear a low, sad moan. Leaning toward her, I kiss her neck and slowly push her down onto the couch.

"Tucker," she breathes. "What are we doing?"

I lick my way along her jaw and meet her gaze. "Kiss me, Sunshine, and let me spoil you."

Without waiting for an answer, I kiss her hard and unrelentingly. She grabs my waist and squeezes, pulling me closer. I'm rock hard against her, and I groan, shifting my hips. She gasps and breaks our kiss.

"Please," she pants.

"Please what?"

"Please touch me."

I palm her breast, kneading it in my hand. She moans, so responsive to my touch. Her hips buck under me, and I growl.

"You need to stop that."

Her bright eyes shine in the dimly lit room. "Or what?"

"Or you'll unleash the beast, and I won't go easy." I smirk as I climb off her. She pouts and sits on the other end of the couch.

With the threat still dangling between us, Lizzy stands up and takes off her shirt to reveal a red lace bra. "One of us is more dressed than the other. That's a problem," she says. She tugs down her shorts, leaving the matching panties on.

I reach my hand out for hers and pull it down to my throbbing cock. "This is what you do to me. Unless you're ready to make good on it, put your clothes back on."

She squeezes my cock in response, eliciting a long groan from my lips. Quickly, I pull her arm and throw her over my lap. A loud crack reverberates through the room as my hand smacks down on her ass. She cries out, stunned.

I do it again. Her cry turns to a low moan as I rub the burning area. "Oh, Lizzy. You've been a bad girl." My hand comes down on her ass again. I dip my hand between her legs, and she jerks against me. I chuckle as I feel how wet she is. "You like this, don't you?"

"Yes, Sir." Lizzy moans loudly as I breach her opening with my finger. "Fuck."

"You have no idea what you do to me, but you're about to find out." My voice is rough with need. I withdraw my finger from her pussy.

"Don't stop, please." She's panting; writhing. My hand comes down again, and she squeals and jerks. "Tucker, *please.*"

"Get on your knees and face me." She climbs off my lap and sits on her knees before me. I've never seen a more beautiful sight, and I didn't think I could get any harder, but I do. My cock is straining against my pants, begging to be freed. I undo my fly and pull my cock out, then grab the base in my hand and stroke it while I look at her. "Tap me three times, for any reason at all, and I'll stop. It all stops."

Her eyes widen. She nods expectantly and leans forward. I reach for her, bending to bring her in for a deep kiss. Lizzy is the most sinfully beautiful thing I have ever tasted, and I've barely begun. Breaking our kiss, I guide her head to the tip of my cock, glistening with pre-cum. She sticks out her tongue and swirls it, moaning in appreciation. My cock twitches and she takes more of me in her mouth. I fist her hair but let her set the pace, and she takes as much of my cock as she can and looks up at me.

"What a good girl." I wink at her. She smiles and starts to bob her head up and down. I can't take much more of this. I shove her head down, forcing her to gag on my cock. When I bring her back up to catch her breath, I wait for the taps. Nothing. "Oh, you like this too." She opens her eyes. They're watering, filled with lust, and I force her head back down, sliding deep into her throat.

I groan. "Oh fuck, Lizzy." She sucks me a little more before I pull her off.

"That mouth. Where have you been hiding it? Goddamn." I'm panting with need. "I never knew how cute you looked with something dirty in your mouth."

She giggles as she teases me with her finger, dragging it up and down my cock.

I stand up, and she whines. "Where are you going?"

"I'm not going anywhere. You are." I step out of my pants. "On the couch, on your knees, facing away from me. I want to see that ass."

Lizzy climbs onto the couch and leans over the back, her tits dangling over the top. I come up behind her and unhook her bra. "Oh, my. These tits are gorgeous," I say over her shoulder. I kiss her neck and grab one of her tits, then pinch her nipple between my fingers. She whimpers.

"You are not to move from this position, no matter what." I let go and take a step back. Her body turns, and I smack her ass hard. "I said don't move."

"Yes, Sir." Her voice is dripping with need.

I groan. "I love it when you call me sir." My fingers dip into her wet pussy, and she moans.

"Fuck. Tucker, don't stop."

I pump my fingers in and out a few times, then withdraw them to stroke my cock with her wetness.

"Remember, three taps and we stop." I line my cock up to her entrance and wait for her nod. The second her head moves, I thrust into her.

She cries out. I grab her hips and fuck her into the couch. It moves beneath us, sliding a little across the floor.

"You're so fucking tight, Lizzy." My cock twitches inside her, and I know I'm almost there. This is better than I could have imagined. I've dreamed of fucking Lizzy and claiming her as mine for years.

Her moans brighten the dark room, making my heart swell. There's a hunger inside of me, begging to be released. This one night won't be enough. She's mine now. All mine.

She reaches back and touches my arm. I catch her arm and twist it behind her back, holding it in place.

"Tucker!"

"Yes, come for me."

She shakes her head.

I stop mid-thrust. "What is it?" I wait for the taps.

"Choke me," she whispers. "Take my air and replace it with you."

Goddamn. She was made for me. A perfect match.

She's all the sunshine I'll ever need.

I thrust back into her, and she gasps. Holding on to the arm behind her back, I straighten her body against mine. I wrap my other hand around her throat and apply a small amount of pressure. She moans and bucks against me.

"You're so beautiful." I squeeze her throat a little more, releasing her arm so I can reach around to touch her clit. Her body jerks. "So responsive to my touch." I rub her clit a little faster, and her breath quickens. I tighten my hand a little more, and she moans.

"Please," she begs. "Please."

"Such a dirty girl." I kiss her shoulder and thrust into her. "Come for me, Lizzy."

She comes undone within my grasp. I slow my thrusts and let her ride it out. "Take it, baby. That's it, Sunshine."

Fuck. Her orgasm brings me so much pleasure. There's nothing hotter than watching her face when she comes. My movement stills as my cock twitches, releasing hot, sticky cum inside of her.

Releasing my grip on her throat, I wrap my arms around her and lay us down on the couch. I grab the discarded blanket and pull it over us. I smooth her hair back, then wrap my arm around her body and pull her close, and we cuddle while I listen to the rise and fall of her chest. Cuddles are the best type of aftercare.

"Go to sleep, Lizzy."

"Tuck . . ." Her voice trails off as her breathing evens out.

I admire the scene before me. Lizzy and I wrapped up in a warm blanket, a fire blazing in the fireplace, a discarded pizza box, and an empty bottle of whiskey. I couldn't be happier than I am right now.

The abandoned house continues to hold happy memories within its floorboards and walls, showing a loving family in its past and welcoming the prospect of a new family. Despite all its flaws, it shows promise and the possibility of miracles.

Chapter Six

BLINDED BY SUNSHINE IS the absolute worst way to wake up. My head pounds against the backs of my eyes, and I wince in pain.

A voice comes from across the room. "Oh, good. You're awake."

Sitting up, I search for the voice. Tucker.

Oh shit. I look down to confirm. *Yep, I'm naked. What have I done?*

"Tucker," I start.

He interrupts me. "Stop. Take this." He hands me two Tylenol and a bottle of water.

I swallow the pills and drink half the bottle. "Oh my god, thank you. I definitely needed that. The sun is so bright." Tucker laughs, and my heart catches in my throat. *My throat. Fuck.* I search for the blanket and pull it up to cover me.

"Don't cover yourself, Lizzy." He shakes his head and kneels down in front of me. "I like you better naked." He smirks.

"Tucker . . . we can't do this." My head hangs low. I can't meet his gaze.

"Yes, we can, and we should." He reaches for my hand, but I pull it away.

"No, we can't. We were drunk and I was sad. I can't lose you, I won't."

"You won't lose me," he says. "Look at me."

I can't.

"Now," he demands.

My eyes slowly meet his, and all I see is lust. It makes it difficult to breathe.

"You'll never lose me, Lizzy. I promise you."

I shake my head. "No. You're my best friend."

"You didn't use the taps last night," he says curiously. "You must like it rough."

I mumble under my breath, "You have no idea."

He pulls me in for a kiss. His kisses make me forget my words, forget everything. I moan into his kiss, letting the blanket fall around me. He pushes me back into the couch and spreads my legs with his body. A cool breeze hits me, but my body is on fire. Tucker ignites something inside me I'm not sure will ever go away.

He trails his fingers up my leg, sending shivers down my spine. Never breaking our kiss, he finds me already soaking wet. He dips a finger into my pussy and moans. His moans are the sexiest thing I've ever heard.

His words break our kiss and leave me panting. "Your pussy is so wet for me. It loved my cock last night." He twists his finger in and out, then adds another one. "Look at it now. My fingers slide in so easily. Fuck, see how you glisten." He removes his fingers to show me just how wet I am. My head falls back, and I'm already high with arousal.

We shouldn't be doing this, but when he kisses me like that, I forget my own name. I can't think of anything else but him. Tucker consumes me. With just a couple of fingers in my pussy, I'm ready to come. I'm on the edge, ready and willing, and that scares me. I can't lose my best friend.

Tucker brings his fingers to his mouth and sucks. "Mmm. You taste good too." There's wicked desire in his eyes, and I'm so far gone that I don't realize what I'm doing. I grab his hand and lick the rest of myself off him. He groans. "Baby, don't start something you don't want to finish."

My body is primed and ready. With his fingers in my mouth, I swirl my tongue around, tasting and teasing every spot I can. His other hand trails up my leg. My back arches, and he plunges his fingers back inside me. He's pumping hard and fast, and I'm still sucking his fingers. I moan around them and spread my legs wider. He adds a third finger, leaving me gasping for air. Saliva drips down my chin, and he slowly pulls his fingers from my mouth, tracing my lips.

"So goddamn beautiful." Then he unbuttons his pants, and I gasp.

Fuck. Shit. Dammit. We should not be doing this. I lick my lips, unable to tell him to stop. There's a war going on inside my head, and right now, all I need is Tucker.

He makes a V shape with the fingers in my pussy and guides his cock to my entrance. My breath hitches, and I wait. Slowly, he slides his cock in between his fingers, and stops.

"Fuck. I feel so—"

"Full?" He laughs, leaving his fingers where they are but thrusting his hips. His fingers stretch me as he plunges deeper inside my pussy. He removes his fingers, grabs my hips, and scoots me down on the couch closer to him. He hooks one of my legs around his waist and puts the other over his shoulder. "Three taps."

I nod, and he captures me in a breath-stealing kiss. He feels so good, so deep. I'm getting closer. I rub my clit to relieve some of the pressure.

Tucker breaks our kiss, growling. "You don't touch yourself unless I say so. Understand?"

"Yes," I whimper.

"Yes, what?" He slaps my inner thigh.

"Ah! Yes, Sir!" My thigh stings and starts to redden.

"Good girl." He grips my throat. "Fuck, you are so beautiful—my hand around your throat, my cock in your pussy, and my name on your lips." He reaches down with his other hand to rub my clit. "This is only for me. Your body is mine." He flicks my clit, causing me to jump.

"Yours," I whisper. My heart sinks, knowing it's the heat of the moment.

He applies more pressure to my throat and continues to fuck me relentlessly. "Your pussy is so tight, made for me."

I'm so close. My breath hitches, and I pinch my nipple between my fingers. I need something extra to throw me over the edge.

All his movements stop.

"No, don't stop! I'm so close. Please," I beg.

"I said no touching. Your pleasure belongs to me now. Tell me what you need."

Removing my hand, I close my eyes because I'm not sure I want to see his face when I ask for what I need. Something Ethan would never give me—pain mixed with pleasure. "Bite me."

No questions asked, he leans down and takes my breast into his mouth. His tongue swirls around my nipple, making it pucker. His movements start again, and then he grips my throat and bites my nipple hard.

It sends an electric shock through my body. I'm shaking uncontrollably as my orgasm crashes through me.

"That's it. You're such a good girl," he says, releasing my nipple.

The look on his face is one of pure lust. There's no hidden agenda, no judgment, no ulterior motive. It's just us.

I haven't fully come down from my high when I feel the pressure building again. "Damn, Tucker. You feel so good. Please don't stop."

"Oh, I'm not done with you yet." He brings his hand to my hip and grips it tightly. With his other hand still around my throat, he fucks me harder. I know he's going to leave bruises. As he switches between light pressure and a heavier hold, my orgasm approaches quickly. I arch my back, and before I can even say a word, Tucker's face is right there. Licking my breast, lightly biting, sucking on my nipple. He teases me so much. I'm panting and right at the edge again.

"Fuck, I'm going to come." I'm getting lightheaded; everything is so intense. My body shivers. Tucker latches on to me, biting my nipple hard. I cry out his name as the orgasm courses through my body.

He doesn't let up. He keeps fucking me into tomorrow and doesn't let go.

"Tucker . . ." I say his name again and try to pull him closer. He's still biting my nipple, and my breath catches in my throat. "Oh, god." The harsh bite of his teeth is better than any clamps I've ever used.

He's pounding into me as another orgasm flows through me. I don't think I've ever come again so soon. My nipple is still between his teeth, and he releases it, only to bite down again.

"Ohhhh." I'm moaning and bucking against him. I can't stop shaking. I can't breathe. The room spins. He bites me one more time, and the whole world comes crashing down.

My whole body tenses, releases, and then goes slack, right as his orgasm rips through him.

"Lizzy. Oh, baby." His body is soft against mine; his head still between my breasts. Slowly, he slides out of me, revealing a sticky mess and leaving me feeling empty yet warm, wrapped up in his arms.

In the harsh light of the day, everything seems so fucked up, especially when the orgasms disappear and all I'm left with is something I'm not sure I should be feeling.

Chapter Seven

Tucker

NEED MIXED WITH WHISKEY is a dangerous potion.

It's been a week since I've heard from her. No texts, no phone calls. An agonizingly long week—probably the longest we've ever gone without talking. I had the best sex of my life. With my best friend. My best friend is not talking to me because she's afraid.

Afraid of getting hurt. Afraid of losing me. Afraid of wanting to be loved the way she knows I'd love her. Lizzy seems tough on the outside, but she's always been soft. It's just who she is.

That's what makes her perfect for me, as evidenced by the dirty, nasty, rough sex. She was born to be a submissive—to be my submissive. She just doesn't know it yet.

I've replayed last weekend a million times in my head. She was so responsive to my touch, and we felt completely in sync. Until I gave her the best orgasm of her life. Until she said we couldn't do this. Until she decided to walk away, and I let her.

Mind-blowing, earth-shattering sex aside, part of me knew it was coming, which is why I have a plan. Her scavenger hunt isn't over yet.

I'm aching to hear her voice. Scrolling through my phone, I hover over her picture when I reach it as I stare at her face. I am wholeheartedly in love with my best friend. I press the call button and wait. It rings, then goes to voicemail. *Okay. Texting it is.*

Me: Hey! I haven't heard from you. Is everything okay?

Lizzy: I don't want to talk right now.

Me: There are a million other things I'd rather be doing, and talking is not one of them.

Lizzy: ...

Lizzy: No, we can't. And I need you to leave it alone.

Me: Your wish is my command.

Lizzy: Thank you.

Me: Thank you, what?

Lizzy: We're not doing this.

Me: Thank you, what?

Lizzy: Thank you, Sir. Now, goodbye.

Me: Such a good girl. Just because we turned it sexual doesn't mean you get to stop saying it. If you stop, there will be consequences.

Lizzy: Okay. :p

Me: You were warned. Why must you tease me?

Lizzy: It's fun to see you riled up.

Me: You haven't seen anything yet.

This woman has absolutely no idea how her words affect me. She deserves to be cherished and loved like no other. She's mine—always has been, always will be.

I palm my cock, willing the hunger to go away. The need to take her is overwhelming. The only thing I regret is that I waited so long. Never mind that it was Ethan who drove her into my arms. Never mind that we were each other's first kiss. Never mind a lot of things.

To be honest, I didn't plan for it to happen this way. I didn't plan for Ethan to cheat, or for us to get drunk and have sex. Ethan's cheating was the catalyst to the drunken sex, that's all.

And I don't regret a single moment of it.

As much as I hate the guy, she was happy. All I've ever wanted was for her to be happy. But damn if I didn't think about standing up at the altar and sweeping her off her feet.

Well, now I don't have to. I have the chance to sweep her off her feet all on my own.

The house at the end of the scavenger hunt isn't the end. The countdown will continue until we descend into madness, and all that's left is me and her.

She leaves me on read, but I pick up my phone and text her back.

Me: What's going on in that pretty head of yours?

Her reply is almost immediate.

Lizzy: Our new client is stopping by the office today, and I'm nowhere near ready.

Me: You'll kill it. My girl always does.

Lizzy: Your girl?

Me: My good girl.

Lizzy: Tucker. We can't do this.

Lizzy: I can't.

Me: That's not what you were saying when you screamed my name.

Lizzy: …

Me: The dirty things I want to do to you. Your loss!

Without waiting for a reply, I click the screen off and set the next part of my plan in motion. T-minus three weeks until her vacation, and it'll be the best vacation of her life. She just doesn't know I hijacked her plans yet.

Chapter Eight

Lizzy

One week later...

The doorbell rings, knocking me out of my trance.
I look down at my new house key and twirl it in my
fingers. With a sigh, I set down the key and walk toward
the front door.

I'm not expecting anyone, especially at this hour. It's
too early in the morning for visitors. Peering through
the peephole, I see someone I don't recognize, wearing
a blue uniform of some kind and holding a rather large
box.

"Hello?" I crack the door.

"Are you Lizzy?"

"Who's asking?"

"These are for you." He sets the package down. "Have a great day, ma'am."

I open the door wider and look around. A white van with flowers on the side is pulling away from the sidewalk. A florist?

The package before me is tall and rectangular. Curious, I bend down and pick it up, noting a silver envelope with the number three on it. I ignore the package and tear into the envelope.

Another card. I turn it over to find another clue.

What the fuck?

Your countdown continues. Need a second to think about this clue? I'll give you some time to find me. While I wait, stay a minute and smell the roses.

A small laugh escapes me. Roses? I untie the blue ribbon on the package and open it up. The package contains a dozen long-stemmed roses.

Roses aren't my favorite flower, but something pulls in my chest when I realize what the clue said. "Stay a minute and smell the roses." My mom's voice rings in my ears; that's something she'd say to me when I was in a hurry to get somewhere.

Lifting the box to my nose, I inhale the familiar scent of freshly cut roses. A wave of emotion crashes into me as I remember fun times giggling with my mom. Blinking furiously to keep the tears at bay, I collect the box and close the door behind me.

The new clue taunts me as I set it by the key. Another countdown? Color me intrigued. I fix myself a cup of coffee, trying to ignore both objects on my table.

A whirlwind of thoughts invades the quiet, so I turn on my playlist to drown out the noise and start dancing. After a couple of songs, Cyndi Lauper starts playing, and it hits me.

Oh my god. The clock! Countdown. Second. Time. Minute.

It's the clock on the tower outside of the fire station. The building reminds me of Big Ben with its old architecture.

Me: Is this you?

I snap a picture of the clue and send it to Tucker.

Tucker: A clue?

Me: Yes.

Tucker: I thought the clues took you to the house. What's this?

Me: You tell me.

Tucker: I think it's a riddle.

Me: Well, duh. Did you send it?

Tucker: To you?

Me: Why are you so frustrating today?

Tucker: Are you always so feisty in the mornings?

Me: Tucker!

Tucker: Yes, my good girl?

Me: Stop.

Tucker: You won't be saying that when you're coming all over my cock.

"Ugh!" I groan. *This is ridiculous.* I know it's him. It has to be!

Me: Who the fuck is sending me clues?

Tucker: Why are you asking me?

Me: Because it's you!

Tucker: No idea what you're talking about. Now be a good girl and come see me.

I leave him on read again for the second time in as many weeks and start pacing through my living room. He's being vague, and rude, and so frustrating!

We could never work as a couple. Someone would eventually get hurt. I've already lost so much; I couldn't bear to lose him too.

Pain flicks through my heart at the mere thought of Tucker leaving.

But what if . . .

What if the best sex of my life could happen all the time? He knew exactly what I needed. And I liked it. I craved it. I need more.

Nope, can't go there.

Needing to get out of the house, I grab my keys and head toward my car.

The fire station is just outside of the plaza. It's a beautiful day, with families everywhere. Kids play in the grass, and parents walk around the winding paths or sit on the benches.

I make my way to the clock tower and see a bundle of balloons tied to the plaque that tells the story of the tower. I'm not sure what pulls me toward the balloons, but when I approach them, there's a brown envelope with the number two on it taped to the string. With every inch I advance, my heart thumps harder.

Still, I know nothing about who is behind this. Of course, I lean toward thinking it's Tucker because he's acting so cagey. He's my best friend and knows everything there is to know about me. Well, almost everything.

He'll never know about my deepest, darkest desires, even if he had a glimpse of it last week. The way I crave to be owned and used. The way I want to be loved and cared for. Ethan didn't know these things, either—he'd never let me show him.

I peel the envelope away from the tape and tear it open.

Sweet and sugary is how you like it. With me, you can get a dozen or more. I'll always have your favorite waiting for you. Get ready to be amazed.

Sweet and sugary? That can only mean one thing: Sweet Apples Bakery. Outside of The Twilight Club, Crimson is known for the absolute best double-fudge brownies. Annie is the sweetest woman too; she's been baking since her early childhood.

I glance at my phone to check the time and realize Tucker should still be at his office. I need him to admit that he's behind the scavenger hunt before I continue.

A shrill voice comes from behind me as I walk into the building. "Lizzy? What are you doing here?"

"You need to leave me alone before you end up with stitches." I walk straight into Tucker's office.

He leans against the front of his desk with an amused expression on his face. "Stitches?"

I shrug. "She's lucky it would only be stitches." I close the door behind me. Kristie is not a part of this conversation.

A low laugh falls from Tucker's mouth. "What brings you by?"

I pull the two envelopes from my back pocket and shove them in his face. "These."

He gives me a puzzled look as he takes the envelopes. "More clues?"

"Why are you sending me on another scavenger hunt? Wasn't the house enough?"

"What are you talking about?"

"You know what I'm talking about. Come on."

He smirks and sets the cards on his desk. "Tsk. Lizzy, isn't the whole point of a scavenger hunt to have fun?"

"Well, yes, but you're also supposed to know who's leaving the clues."

"Are you?"

"Aren't you?" I challenge. "I know it's you, I just need you to admit it."

"There's nothing to admit." He stalks toward me.

I take a step back but am forced to stop when my back hits the door. "Tucker," I say breathily as he grabs my wrists and pins them above my head with one hand.

"Giving you the house isn't enough," he whispers in my ear. "Nothing will ever be enough." He trails his tongue down my neck, and my breath hitches as his other hand grabs my waist.

"Tucker." It's a warning and a plea.

He nibbles on my neck, then moves his mouth back to my ear. "The only thing that will be close to enough is my cock buried inside you until you scream over and over again."

I try to turn my head away, but he stops me.

"Don't look away from me, Sunshine," he commands.

Every inch of my body is aching to comply. I meet his gaze and gasp. *Holy shit.* The lust in his eyes is consuming. He lets go of my waist to cup my cheek. It's such a tender touch, it takes me by surprise.

My mouth opens to speak, but nothing comes out. Tucker seizes the opportunity to take my bottom lip into his mouth and suck on it. I moan before I can stop myself. He deepens our kiss, replacing his tender touch with something else entirely.

His tongue enters my mouth as I pull him closer. Lost in the sensations, I don't realize he's lifted my leg around his waist until he grinds against me, making me feel how much he wants me.

Tucker growls and breaks our kiss, leaving me panting. "I will own you, my sweet Lizzy. You will be on your knees begging for my cock like a good girl."

I squirm against him and feel him grow harder. "We can't."

"You will be mine. All mine." He bruises my lips with his rough kiss like I'm what he needs to survive.

A knock on the door interrupts us, and the shrill voice rings out again. "Your eleven o'clock is here."

"Be right there," Tucker says to Kristie from behind the closed door. He leans into my ear again. "I bet you're soaking wet for me." His fingers trail up my leg to my hot center, and he chuckles.

"Tucker, we—" He cuts me off as he rubs his finger over the fabric of my pants. I swallow hard, forgetting the rest of my words.

My hips involuntarily buck against him. "Mmm, needy girl." His lips meet my neck, and he gently bites, then sucks to relieve the ache. He repeats the motions over and over. I know it's going to leave a mark.

His hand grazes the skin above my pants, and I draw in a quick breath. He dips his hand under my waistband, his palm hot against my skin, and the touch pulls a low groan from me.

Tucker tightens his grip on my wrists, reminding me they're still pinned above my head. "Not one sound, Lizzy."

I shake my head and try to pull my hands down, but he's too strong for me. As his finger slides through my wet folds and into me, he bites down on my neck again. I gasp, using my leg to pull him closer.

He licks my neck to soothe the spot he bit. "See? So wet." He slides his finger in and out, taking his time, then slowly adds a second.

Another knock startles me. "Tucker, you're late."

"Just a sec!" He gives me a wicked smile. His fingers continue to move inside me, and the pressure starts to build.

We shouldn't be doing this. My mind and my body are telling me two different things. Tucker bites down again, knowing the exact amount of pressure I need. My hips buck, trying to match the pace of his fingers.

It's all too much. The war is splitting me in half, and my body gives in to the affection. I'm panting, gasping for breath, as I come apart in Tucker's hand.

His movements slow down as I ride out my orgasm. "That's my good girl," he murmurs against my neck.

I'm coming down from my high when I realize he's released my wrists and is carrying me across the room to the comfy chair I love—the one I picked out for him when he got this office a few years ago. He picks up the blanket hanging on the back of the couch and quickly covers me with it. Then he walks over to his mini-fridge, pulls out a bottle of water, and hands it to me.

"I need to go, but take your time. You can leave when you're ready." He kisses my forehead and walks out of the office, leaving me alone to process what just happened.

Chapter Nine

Tucker

IT'S NOT LONG BEFORE I see Lizzy walking out of the building. She's flushed and rushing out the front door like she's doing the walk of shame.

I discreetly readjust my cock under the table, willing it to go away. All I can think about is dominating her. Molding her, cradling her, forcing her to take my cock. Making love to her, hearing her scream my name. I want all that and a bag of chips.

"Tucker?"

"Ah, yes. Sorry. You were saying?"

"We'd like to do the walk-through first, then meet up for the closing. Is that all right?"

"Of course, yes. I'm excited to see this through closing. The property is beautiful; you'll love it there." I smile at the young couple sitting across the table from me. "I'll meet you guys at the house tomorrow afternoon."

We stand up, ending the meeting. I walk them out, hoping to catch a glimpse of Lizzy. My heart sinks a little when her car is gone.

Walking back into the office, I pull out my phone and send her a message.

Me: Every piece of me aches for you.

Lizzy: Did you send me the clues?

Me: I think about you when you're not here.

Lizzy: Stop it. This is dumb, just tell me.

Me: You are intoxicating, Lizzy.

Lizzy: You are irritating.

Me: Feisty, just the way I like you.

Lizzy: I'm ignoring you now.

Me: You can't ignore the pull between us. One taste is not enough, it never will be.

Lizzy: We're not talking about us. I'm asking you about the clues.

Me: Just go with it.

Lizzy: No! I'm tired of you dodging the question!

Me: I meant with the clues.

Me: You'll enjoy the journey and where it leads.

Me: Finish the scavenger hunt, Lizzy.

A smile flashes across my face as I think about where she's going. She's heading to our favorite bakery, where delicious treats await her.

For the next couple of hours, I bury myself in the mountain of paperwork on my desk. I have two other closings this week, in addition to the one tomorrow. No matter the size of the town, there's always a need for realtors who can sell houses.

My phone dings twice. I fumble around trying to find it, only to find it under a stack of papers.

Lizzy: Hi

Lizzy: (Incoming picture)

Me: Mouth-watering, aren't they?

Lizzy: These are so good.

Me: Well, they are your favorite. Don't forget to save me one!

Lizzy: As if! These babies are all mine.

Me: You're going to be sorry you said that.

Lizzy: No, Sir. I don't think I will be.

Me: Just you wait.

Me: Did you get another clue?

Lizzy: Did I?

Lizzy: (Incoming picture)

You've been there once for a clue. So now go back to the place you've never been.

Me: Where might that be?

Lizzy: Can we meet?

Me: Sure, your place? I'm just about done here.

Lizzy: That's fine.

There's just one clue left. If it's wrong for my heart to skip a beat knowing where she's going, then I don't want to be right.

Chapter Ten

Lizzy

No matter how hard I try, I can't deny the spark between us. I've tried to argue against being with him. I've tried to talk myself out of it, tried to convince myself nothing good can come of it.

But when I listen to my heart, it whispers his name.

I get those butterflies in my stomach, my palms start to sweat, and my heart beats faster. It's like my first crush all over again.

When I listen to my head, it becomes silent.

There are no more thoughts of saying no, no more worries of hurt or rejection, and I don't feel terrified to let him in. A little scared, yes, but who isn't scared at the start of something new?

I pace around the living room, waiting.

I'm used to playing it safe. After my mom died, I wouldn't let anyone get close. Slowly, Tucker melted my icy heart and made me warm again.

There's a knock on the door, and I rush over to open it.

"When did it start raining?" I peer outside behind Tucker.

"What? No hello?" He laughs.

"Sorry, come in."

"I know you love the rain something fierce, but you could at least be happy to see me."

"Shhh. I'm always happy to see you. But the rain will always win," I tease.

He closes the door behind him and walks into the living room. I move to the window to stare outside. A second later, I feel his presence behind me, but I don't move.

"Lizzy," he whispers in my ear. "Nothing wins against you."

I chuckle and shake my head, leaning back into him. He wraps an arm around my waist. We stand there for a moment in complete silence, watching the rain cascade down the window and into the valley before us. My heart thumps in my chest at the closeness of him. The butterflies in my chest start to flutter because they know what's coming next. I'm nervous as I turn around to face him.

"Tucker, I—"

"I know." He smirks.

I playfully swat his arm. "You don't know anything."

His lips meet mine in the lightest, sweetest kiss I've ever had. I'm waiting for him to pounce, but he doesn't. Our kiss is sensual and loving. There are no expectations around this kiss, it's just us.

After a minute, he pulls away, and I whine. "Oh baby, we're not done yet. Wipe that pout off your face."

He winks and walks into the kitchen.

The storm is coming in strong.

It's as if the lightning recharges my soul, while the rain cleanses it. The thunder comes a second later and resonates deep in my bones. Every ragged piece falls into place.

This is not what I expected when Tucker came over. It wasn't my intention. I wanted to question him where there was nowhere to avoid me and I could finally get some answers.

Instead, I don't question what I do next, because it couldn't be more right. I drop to my knees, place my hands palm-side up on my legs, and bow my head. I close my eyes, take a deep breath, and slowly let it out.

"Well, I'll be damned." His voice drips with desire. I don't dare look up at him. I'm silent as he makes his way around me, circling like I'm prey.

My chest rises and falls with each breath as I wait for something, anything, to tell me what he's thinking.

I've never been in this position before. But all I know is I need him to own me, and all I want to do is please him, any way I can.

My body jerks when his breath hits my ear. "You're a dirty girl. Look at me."

I open my eyes and meet his gaze. Lust swims through my veins, and I see the corresponding fire in his eyes.

"Sir?"

He takes a sharp breath. "There you go again . . ." Tucker mutters. "Are you sure this is what you want, Sunshine?"

An uneasy feeling captures me, and I'm forced to look away.

Tucker reaches out and grabs my chin, returning my gaze to him. "I need an answer, Lizzy."

The answer falls silent on my lips. I open my mouth, but nothing comes out.

"If we go down this road, there is no going back. I will own you, for better or worse. Your orgasms are mine, your needy, wet cunt is mine, and you will be mine."

My body shivers with his words. "Yes," I breathe.

He raises an eyebrow. "Yes, what?"

"Yes, Sir." The response is immediate.

"This is going to be fun." He releases my chin and trails his hand down my neck to my arm, then to my hand, and draws circles on my palm with his finger. "There are three main rules you must obey at all times. One: don't deny me. I can have you anytime I want. Two: you don't come until I say you do. You will ask my permission to orgasm every time. And three: communicate with me often. Use the safeword and everything will stop, no questions asked. Your limits will be tested, you will be punished, and you will enjoy every agonizingly blissful moment."

His eyes stare into mine, and all the uneasy feelings fall away. I nod. "Safeword?" I ask.

"Skittles," he says.

A loud laugh escapes me.

"Skittles? That's the best you can come up with?" I stick my tongue out, and he tilts his head.

"Okay, so that's what you want to focus on? Let's shift your focus to what you just did."

"And what's that?" I ask.

"You're taunting me. Already." His smile turns into a wicked grin. "Bad girls get punished; good girls get to come."

A nervous laugh escapes before I can stop it.

"Oh, darling. You won't be laughing in a minute. It's a good thing I grabbed some water when I was in the kitchen. You're going to need it." He stands up and backs away from me, takes off his coat, and unbuckles his belt.

"Take off your shirt and pants. Leave the rest on and resume the position."

I stand and quickly take off my clothes. Once I'm standing in my bra and underwear, I kneel back down and place my hands on my knees, spreading them slightly apart.

"Good girl," he murmurs and walks toward me. "This is going to be fast and hard. You have no idea how long I've been waiting for this moment—the moment where you submit to me and become mine." Lust drips from his words, igniting the fire inside my body.

Tucker kneels down in front of me and touches my chin. Instinctively, I look up at him. He leans into me and kisses me. It's not like the kiss we had earlier. This one is possessive—marking his territory. I'm lost in his kiss. I'm lost in the thought of us.

The touch of his hand on my underwear jolts my body. He breaks the kiss to speak against my lips. "Look at this. Your underwear is soaked, and I've barely touched you." He adds pressure to my clit through the wet fabric, and I moan. "Mmm. That's a sweet sound."

I'm panting as he rubs the bundle of nerves between my legs. "Please."

"Please what?" His movements stop.

"Sir. Please touch me, Sir."

"Oh, like this?" In a swift second, he cups my pussy with his palm and shoves two fingers inside my folds.

"Yes!" I pant.

Our lips meet again, his fingers pump inside me, and I'm so close. It's like Tucker can read my body, though, because he slows his fingers.

"Don't stop," I whimper. "Please."

He withdraws his fingers and reaches up to trace my lips. My tongue snakes out to lick the tip of his finger. He allows me this small taste before he drags my wetness down my body and back to my slick pussy.

"You're not allowed to come yet, baby." He dips his fingers inside me again, and I sigh with relief.

The moment he withdrew from me, I felt empty. I never knew I could feel that way, especially about my best friend.

Tucker picks up his pace, and then slows down again. He repeats the back-and-forth motion. *Oh fuck, he is skilled. What have I gotten myself into?*

I moan as he starts to go faster. Sex permeates the air, and we've barely begun.

With his other hand, he unhooks my bra and lets it fall down my arms. I start to catch it to help pull it off, but he puts a hand on my arm. I stand still as his fingers slowly tease their way inside my pussy. Then he drags them out and pushes them back in, and then makes a circling motion.

"You are not to move your hands or I will tie them up."

Not trusting my words, I nod. *This is going to be difficult.*

He leans down and takes my breast into his mouth. His tongue swirls around my nipple, then he gently bites down and rolls it between his teeth.

"Fuck," I hiss.

There's a popping sound as he releases his hold on my breast. He drags his tongue around my breast, then slowly teases the other one. His fingers are still moving at an agonizingly slow pace, tormenting me and teasing me with an orgasm.

I'm on edge, ready to tip at a moment's notice.

"Lizzy," he groans against my skin. "Mmm. Your cunt is so needy. The way it's sucking in my fingers each time . . ."

The fire starts to burn brighter. I'm not sure how much longer I'll last. "Please, Sir."

"Please what?"

"May I come, please?"

A wicked laugh is not what I expect to hear. "In a moment. I need something first."

"Anything." I pant.

I feel myself stretch as he adds another finger, and I shift my hips, allowing him deeper inside me.

"You're not allowed to move for three minutes. Do that, and your wish is my command."

Easy. "Okay."

"No matter what."

His fingers move slowly inside me while he leans down to lick my neck. I groan and lean into the sensation. All of his movements come to a halt.

"Poor, sweet girl," he mocks. "You moved."

"I'm sorry! Please don't stop." *Shit.*

"That wasn't even thirty seconds! I guess a little punishment is in order."

My eyes widen. "What? No, I'm sorry!"

"Oh yes," he chuckles. "You will sit absolutely still for one full minute, and you will count it out. Go."

I raise my eyebrow.

"Make it ninety seconds."

I start counting. "One, two, three, four . . ." I half expected him to move his fingers again, but his hand is a statue. It's all I can do to not move my hips. There are three fingers in my pussy. I feel so full, and I need to move.

When I get to forty-five seconds, he takes me in his mouth again and flicks his tongue against my puckered nipple. At sixty seconds, he bites down hard.

The bite takes my breath away. I quickly recover and resume counting. He doesn't let go of my nipple until I get to eighty seconds. Then he switches back to licking it.

"Eighty-seven, eighty-eight, eighty-nine."

I'm not able to say ninety because my reward comes swift and fast. He bites my nipple again and pumps his fingers in and out so fast and hard that I instantly come undone.

"Fuck. Tucker!" Those fingers don't slow as I ride out my orgasm. "Oh, fuck."

"That's my good girl." His voice is in my ear, calming me. My heart races. I can't breathe.

Everything around me fades away as he wraps his arms around me, leaving me wondering what the fuck just happened and why I liked it so much.

Chapter Eleven

Tucker

LIZZY IS THE MOST stunning woman on the planet. I grab the blanket and drape it over us, then pull her closer to me, resting her head on my shoulder. I'm stroking her hair while I listen to her breathing even out.

"Here, drink this." I uncap the bottle of water and hand it to her. She desperately takes the bottle and tips it up to her mouth. "One more sip." She does as asked and hands the bottle back to me, then sighs and wiggles against me to get more comfortable.

"You good?"

"Perfect. That was . . ."

"Amazing?"

She tilts her head up to look at me. "Beyond amazing. I've never had an orgasm that strong before."

"Ah, you're so perfect."

"You're not so bad yourself." She laughs. I've heard it a million times before, but somehow, it's different this time. It's more light and carefree, but still teasing and loving.

I run my hand up her arm, teasing her ever so slightly. She shivers at my touch. "Ready for more?"

"Wait, you're not wearing a shirt." I shake my head. "And you took my bra off!"

"Oh, yes, I did. Free the titties!" She laughs with me.

"Are we really doing this?"

"As long as you want this. For so long, it's been you."

"What about the other girls?"

"Nah, that was just sex—nothing more. It never would be. But with you? It's more than sex."

She shifts a little and puts her arm around my waist, stroking my side. My cock stirs under the blanket.

"The way you knelt before me with no idea as to how I would react? That's the woman who stole my heart. The woman who acts without regret. Shit, I almost grabbed you and fucked you into oblivion. You looked amazing, but I wanted to play with you."

"Tucker," she whispers. "I'm scared."

I kiss her forehead. "I know, baby, I know. I'll take care of you." I grab her hand and guide it down to my cock. It strains against my boxers, begging to be released. "Can you show me how thankful you are for the mind-blowing orgasm?"

She teases my cock by running her finger up and down the shaft. "Oh, yes, Sir." My cock twitches when she calls me that.

"Fuck," I mutter. "Take me in your mouth."

Lizzy lifts herself off me and moves to crouch between my legs. Her tongue darts out, meeting my glistening tip, and I hiss.

She opens her mouth and leans over my cock, barely letting me in. Her lips close around the tip, and she sucks ever so lightly. I reach down and grab the top of her head, lacing my fingers through her hair. As I tighten my grip, she takes more of me in her mouth. She swirls her tongue around the head, then trails down the shaft.

I feel her hands on my thighs and realize she's bracing herself. *My greedy girl.* "Lizzy," I breathe.

She looks up at me, most of my shaft in her mouth.

"You're a dirty girl, aren't you?"

Instead of answering me, she slowly moves her head down the rest of my shaft with a gentle moan and closes her eyes. The tip of my cock hits the back of her throat, causing her to gag. I drag her head back up to let her breathe.

Eyes still closed, I know she's ready. I let her set the pace for a minute while she sucks my cock. It feels so good, I know I'm about to come down her pretty throat, but I'm not done with her yet.

When she comes back up to suck the tip in her mouth, I push her head back down and hold it there. My hips thrust hard, and my cock dips down her throat. She gags but doesn't move. I thrust a few more times, and I'm so close.

"Fuuuuck."

Lizzy opens her glistening eyes and meets my gaze. The moment our eyes meet, my orgasm racks through me. My cock twitches and shoots hot, sticky cum into her mouth. A tear rolls down her face, but she takes it, never breaking eye contact.

She swirls her tongue around my cock and moans, sending a shiver down my spine.

"Damn, you're so greedy for my cum." I chuckle and release her hair. She hasn't stopped licking and sucking my cock, waiting for every last drop of my cum.

Finally, she releases me with a *pop* and smiles, then climbs back over to snuggle in my arms again.

I'm running my fingers through her hair when she speaks.

"Why Skittles?"

"They all taste the same, no matter what the package says. And I hate them." I shrug. I really do hate them.

"So, if I say Skittles . . ."

"Not if, when. When you say Skittles, everything stops because something is wrong. You're in the wrong kind of pain, you don't like what I'm doing. No matter if you're handcuffed to my bed or spread across the desk, we'll immediately stop everything and have a conversation."

"Okay, easy enough."

"I'll push you to your limits and beyond. There's bound to be something you won't like. It's my job to find out where the limit is and what we can do to make everything pleasurable for you."

"Mmm, I like the sound of that." She squeezes the arm draped on my waist, then wraps me in a hug. "What about you, though?"

My phone dings on the coffee table. I reach for it and slide to unlock it. It's a message from my mom. I groan. "Damn it. I'm so sorry, baby." I sit up. She follows with a puzzled look on her face. "I forgot I was supposed to help my mom put up the shelves in the garage today. She's asking when I'll be over."

She rolls her eyes and laughs. "Yeah, you better not keep Amy waiting."

I pull on my pants, captivated by Lizzy's beauty the whole time. I can't seem to look away. "While I'm gone, I need you to do something for me."

"What's that?" She runs her fingers through her messy hair.

"Go get an uncooked lasagna for dinner; tell Milo it's on me. Then, while it's cooking, go take a bubble bath. Finish your scavenger hunt and take your vacation.

Take the time to reflect and make sure this is what you truly want." I motion between us. "I wasn't kidding earlier. If we're doing this, I'm all in. You will be mine, and I will never let you go."

I take a few steps back to the couch and lean down to kiss her. "Promise me you'll do it."

"Yes, Sir."

I groan into her kiss and pull away. "Lizzy."

"Fine, I promise." She waves her hand through the air as if to shoo me away. "You'd better go. Amy's gonna be mad if you're not there soon."

She's right. My mom's "when are you coming over" text means you're at least an hour late.

One more kiss, then I head toward the front door. "I mean it. Punishments will be plenty when you come back if you haven't done what I've asked."

She laughs. "I mean, I'm not going anywhere big. Not anymore. Ethan and I were supposed to go across the border and stay somewhere nice in Colorado to get away. Instead, I'm just taking some quiet time—relaxing at the lake, reading a book or two. I'll still be around, silly boy."

My heart hums with excitement.

Little does she know the surprise that awaits her.

Chapter Twelve

Lizzy

WHEN I GET TO Milo's restaurant, he's assisting a couple I can't make out in the far booth in the back. It's a surprisingly busy night tonight. My eyes wander, and I'm looking for the next clue when I spot Ethan and Kristie.

Oh, the fucking nerve!

I clench my fists at my sides and am about to walk out empty-handed when I spot a manila envelope. Intrigued, I take a deep breath and walk closer to the map. Just like last time, the envelope is pinned to Venice. I don't have to look around to know it's for me. No one else would post things on Milo's map. Or, at least, not without his permission.

The rest of the world melts away as I open the envelope. There are two additional envelopes, both silver.

"Sweet Lizzy!" Milo startles me. I turn around and step into his hug.

"It's good to see you, Milo. How are you?"

He gestures around. "Too busy! The usual?"

"Actually, no. Well, yes—just uncooked, today. I'm under strict instructions to warm it up at home."

"You got it." He smiles and turns to put my order in.

"Oh, before I forget. Tucker said to charge it to his account."

"You've got him wrapped around your little finger, don't you?" He winks and adds, "It'll be out soon."

"What's that supposed to mean?" I wonder out loud as I turn my attention back to the silver envelopes. I open the one with "Lizzy" written in cursive on it.

Congratulations, again! You've reached the end. One more riddle—absolutely do not open the other envelope until you figure it out. Good luck, and have fun.

I'm all around you, yet I remain unseen. I'm not beautiful nor ugly, I'm just in between. Too much time on me can make you fall asleep. We'll have an exciting journey together, but don't peek!

What the? I reread the clue again. Then one more time, trying to make sense of it. I contemplate opening the second envelope in my hand but hear my name behind me.

Spinning around, I come face-to-face with Ethan. I groan and take a step backward.

"Lizzy. How have you been?"

"You don't get to ask me that, Ethan."

"What do you mean?" He flashes me the smile I used to be so fond of.

I grimace as I answer. "Exactly what I said. You don't get to ask me how I'm doing. You don't get to ask me about my life as if nothing happened. You don't get to care or have feelings about the way I picked myself up after you tore me apart."

At the right moment, Milo returns with my dinner. "Here you go, Lizzy. And, of course, there's always a little something extra for you. You deserve it."

My arm reaches out for the lasagna, and I step to the side to move away from Ethan. "Thank you so much, Milo. I appreciate it. See you later."

I'm walking out of the restaurant when I hear Kristie's shrill voice. "You didn't do anything wrong, baby. She's a bitch anyway."

It takes no effort at all to just keep walking. As much as I hate Kristie, I have better things to do.

The playlist I have on is interrupted by a few dings. I hear the water still running in the background, the lasagna is in the oven, and I'm getting ready to soak in the tub. I toss my shirt in the hamper and reach for the phone sitting on my dresser.

Tucker: You better be taking your bath.

Me: (Incoming picture)

Tucker: It would be better with you in it.

Me: Jumping in now, Sir.

Tucker: Good girl.

Heat crawls up my body. I never thought I'd need Tucker's words as much as I'm craving them right now. Before putting my phone down on the counter, I double-check the timer: 45 minutes.

I lower the rest of my body into the warm water and close my eyes. The candles around me flicker in the dark, the sweet scent of vanilla and brown sugar filling the bathroom. My mind flickers back to the scene from earlier.

He looked at me like he wanted to devour me. A sigh falls from my lips as I remember the way he licked and sucked my breasts. Tucker makes me want to do all the things I've ever imagined.

It was so easy to submit to him, to give up that control. To surrender my mind and body to someone. And he accepted it, greedily and loving.

Fuck. The way he masterfully pulled my strings and knew exactly what I wanted, what I needed, before I did.

My fingers roam my body, and I wish they were his fingers stroking me instead. I find my slick entrance and lightly touch myself, adding more pressure each time. My moans fill the room, and before long, I know I'm close. With my other hand, I fumble for my phone. I finally grasp it and press the three buttons that will speed-dial Tucker.

It barely starts to ring before his husky voice comes down the line. "Yes, Sunshine?"

A loud moan comes out instead of words.

"Lizzy," he groans.

"I'm so close. Please, Sir."

"Mmm, you're a dirty girl. Are you still in the tub?"

"Yes," I breathe. My hand still works below the water, and I pinch my nipple between my fingers.

"Are you imagining it's me touching your sweet cunt?"

"Yes. *Fuck.*" I moan again.

"That's right, baby. Imagine my fingers moving in and out of your pussy, your sweet juices running down my hand."

"Tucker," I whimper. "Oh, god."

"Your pussy isn't going to be the only thing I fuck . . . I'm going to fuck that pretty little mouth of yours, and then I'm going to take your tight ass and empty my load inside you. I'm going to use your holes for my pleasure. I'd love to see you a blubbering hot mess."

"P-p-please, Sir."

"Come for me, baby."

I scream his name as I come hard.

"That's my good girl." His voice dips, his need sounding like pure sin, and it's the key to my heart. It's the thing I needed all along, and now, I never want to let him go.

My breaths even out, but when I look back over at my phone, the call is still connected. A blush creeps up my cheeks when I realize I just had phone sex with my best friend.

"Tucker?" I ask, unsure of what comes next.

"Time to get out of the tub. Your dinner awaits."

I pause, a light clicking inside my head.

"It's an airplane!" I blurt out, hearing his laughter.

"What?"

"Oh my god. The last clue is an airplane. Now, what did you do?"

He laughs. "I have no idea what you are referring to."

"Oh, stop being cagey."

"Live a little; enjoy the ride. Bye, Lizzy." He hangs up.

"Ugh!" I roll my eyes and pull up the stopper to drain the water.

Before I climb out of the tub, I blow out the candles and wrap myself in my big, comfy robe. I pull the robe tight and tie it up. The timer dings a second later.

I rush out to the kitchen and open the oven, then set the lasagna on the counter. It smells delicious! I pop the garlic bread in the oven for a minute on a broil and scoop some food onto my plate. Then I place the bread on the plate and snap a picture. It's definitely not social-media worthy, but it's good enough.

Without waiting for a response from Tucker, I put the phone back in my pocket and head to the couch to finish up the latest episode of *Criminal Minds*. Nothing like a bath, an orgasm, amazing food, and serial killers to end my night.

Shit! The envelope. I jump up and find my purse discarded on the bed. Quickly, I open it and pull out the unmarked envelope. I'm careful not to rip this one because I'm not sure of its contents.

A thin piece of paper greets me, and I slide it out to read it. It's a boarding pass with one location listed. Italy.

What the fuck? Italy? Whaaat?

I'm going to Italy! The ticket is dated for this weekend.

When I turn it over, there's a sticky note on the back.

Take an extra week. I've already cleared it with Melanie. Enjoy the pasta and wine!

I quickly grab my phone.

Me: TUCKER!

Me: ANSWER ME NOW.

Tucker: Is that any way to talk to your Sir?

Me: WHAT THE HELL?

Me: You bought me a ticket to Italy?!

Tucker: Oh, you'll have to answer for this when you come back.

Me: Yes, Sir.

Me: WHY DID YOU BUY ME A TICKET TO ITALY?

Tucker: Go have fun, Sunshine. Enjoy your time off. You work hard, and you've dreamt of Italy since before I met you.

Me: I can't believe it.

Me: Thank you so much!

My heart is screaming with happiness. Italy! This is going to be the best vacation ever. How many girls have best friends who would buy them a plane ticket to Italy?

Me: Wait, you're coming with me, right??

Tucker: Not this time. Just don't find some gorgeous Italian man to sweep you off your feet.

Me: We'll see!

Now my heart sinks a little. This is the trip of a lifetime, and my best friend won't be there with me.

I settle back into the couch and press play. Garcia and Morgan's banter is a comforting hum in the background.

I take it back.

There's nothing like a bath, an orgasm, amazing food, serial killers, and a ticket to Italy to end my night.

Chapter Thirteen

Five days later...

Julie sits on my bed, helping me pack. She's advising me on which shoes to bring and the reasons why. I'll need a pair for dancing, one for hiking, and one for shopping, plus my everyday shoes.

That's four pairs of shoes for two weeks. I barely use four pairs of shoes in a month!

My big suitcase is already filled to the brim with sundresses, long and flowy shirts, blouses, some jeans, and a sweater or two. The medium suitcase is what I'm trying to pack right now. It'll have my shoes, toiletrics, and undergarments.

Two weeks is a long time to vacation in another country. I have no idea what I will and won't need on the trip, so I pack a little of everything. Plus, I'll need room for souvenirs—that's what the small suitcase is for. It's currently stuffed into the medium one for maximum portability.

Thunder rumbles through the sky. *What a great day for flying.*

"This is too much." I grunt as I zip up the second suitcase. "It's gotta weigh over the fifty-pound limit."

"I think you're good. If it does, so what? You'll pay the fee and be on your merry way." She shrugs. "I am so freaking jealous, by the way. Moxie is too. We can't believe Tucker bought you a ticket to Italy!"

"I can't either. I've been talking about it for a long time, but I never thought the day would come." I laugh. "It blows my mind that he would do this for me."

Her eyes widen. "Are you serious right now?"

"Yeah, why?"

"Are you fucking blind?" I gape at her. "I mean, obviously, but have you seen the way he looks at you? He's Snow White and you're the apple, except you're not poisoned."

I chuckle and shake my head. "Oh my god."

"I'm not joking. He's been head over heels for you forever. Ever noticed how he's never had a serious girlfriend? He was so pissed when Ethan proposed to you. Come on, you can't tell me you didn't notice he has the hots for you! He loves you, girly."

Her statement causes me to sit down on the bed. "Wow." I can't believe what I'm hearing. It all starts to click into place.

Tucker's in love with me . . . and has been for years.

"Well, shit. That explains why he sent me on a crazy scavenger hunt. First for the house, now this? I can't believe it."

The butterflies flutter in my stomach again. I know exactly what I have to do when I come back.

I've already talked to Tucker this morning, and he's in back-to-back meetings today. I won't be able to talk to him again until I land in Italy. I haven't seen him since the morning I submitted to him. My body is already aching for his touch.

"Now that I've given you something to think about for the next two weeks," Julie says with a smirk, "let's get you to the airport before the storm really picks up."

"Good idea." I nod and stand up, reaching for my purse. "Phone, wallet, passport, phone charger, ChapStick, a book, and my keys. I'm ready."

She helps me bring my luggage to the car and load it in.

"Just in case I haven't said it already, thank you," I say to Julie.

"You don't have to thank me. It's what I'm here for!"

"Still, I appreciate it. I could drive, but I'd rather not leave my car at the airport for two weeks."

"I got you." She climbs into the driver's side of the car and starts it up. I follow, ready for my next adventure.

It doesn't take us long to arrive at the airport. I wave goodbye to Julie, then wheel my two suitcases inside to the line for the ticket counter. There are quite a few people in front of me, surprisingly enough. I know I haven't been to the airport in a while, but it's busier than I expected. Reaching into my back pocket, I pull out my phone and check the time.

Okay, my flight leaves in an hour. I need to get checked in, go through security, hit the bathroom, and grab some snacks. There should be enough time.

The line moves slower than I'd like, but eventually, I'm next in line.

"Ticket and ID?"

"Here you go." I hand both to the ticket agent. He nods and looks over the documents.

While he inspects them, I hoist my suitcases onto the cart so he can tag them.

"And you have your passport, ma'am?"

"Yes, I do." I hand that over as well.

"Thank you." He scans my ticket, then hands all three things back to me. "Have a nice flight."

He moves to secure the tags on the luggage and waves to the next person.

"Next in line!"

"Thank you!" I grab the documents he set on the counter and rush over to the security gates.

There's a long line here too. I take the opportunity to check the time again.

45 minutes until the plane leaves. I can do this.

Thankfully, security moves at a quicker pace than the ticket counter did. I hand the ticket and my ID to the security agent, who scans them again.

She hands them back and motions for me to move through the scanner. I quickly lay my items on the conveyor belt after I pocket my ticket and ID. My shoes are first on the belt, then I lift my backpack up and remove my empty water bottle and my Kindle. After patting my front pockets to make sure they're empty, I step through the scanner.

Beep! Beep!

I look around for a split second before I realize it's beeping at me.

"Check your pockets, miss," a feminine voice says beside me.

I pat my pockets again and my hand hits something hard. "Ugh," I groan as I pull my phone out of my back pocket. The one pocket I didn't check.

"Sorry!"

I toss the phone on the conveyor belt and step through the scanner again.

Silence.

"Thank god," I mutter as I walk over to my belongings at the end of the belt. Someone had pushed them to the end for me like I didn't grab them quick enough.

I shove everything back in my carry-on and slide my shoes on. I'm so glad I wore sandals instead of my tennis shoes.

Walking quickly, I head over to the concessions store. The Crimson Mountain Airport is fairly small, even though it's considered to be a major hub in our little corner. Shoulder to shoulder with other shoppers, I maneuver my way around the store, grabbing a couple of things.

If airports are good for one thing, it's standing in lines.

There are three people in front of me, so I pull out my phone to check the time while I wait.

15 minutes left.

"I can help next in line!" A man's voice cuts through all the white noise and catches my attention.

"Oh, sorry." I hurry to the counter and set the items down, quickly pay for them, and head toward one of the eight gates at the airport.

"Now boarding group C on Flight 1812 to Italy."

I'm in group A, so I have a few more minutes until boarding. My bladder protests as I make my way to the seating area. Internally, I groan. *Better go now before it's too late.*

Outside the bathroom is a small line. I take a deep breath to help calm my anxiety. While I'm not terrified of airplanes, they do make me uneasy. I've seen *Final Destination* one too many times.

No matter how old I am, if someone says they need to get off a plane, I'm going with them. And I will never drive behind a logging truck. Those things scare the shit out of me. Thank you, *Final Destination 2*, for the traumatic story line.

As soon as I come out of the bathroom, I hear the steward over the intercom.

"Last call for Flight 1812 to Italy."

"Shit!" I mumble. *What happened to the time?*

I jog toward the gate and see there are two people scanning their tickets to board the plane.

Out of breath, I pull my ticket out and shove it facedown on the scanner. It beeps and lights up green.

"Just in time, ma'am. Enjoy your flight."

"Thank you!"

I make it to the end of the jetway just as the flight attendant is getting ready to close the door. She hands me a small bag of items and tells me to find my seat. Row 10, Seat A.

Ding. I sit down in my seat as soon as the seatbelt sign turns on.

"Ladies and gentlemen, welcome to Flight 1812 from Crimson to Venice, Italy. We're in for a long flight. Please do let us know if you have any questions after our brief security video. We'll be coming around for beverages shortly. We may have some turbulence as we make our way out of the storm. Please remain seated while the seatbelt sign is on. Thank you and enjoy the flight."

A video starts playing in front of the plane on a big screen. I guess they go all out for international flights. This plane is way fancier than the last one I was on, which was many years ago.

Once I am comfortably seated, or as comfortable as I can be in the aisle seat, I open the small bag and examine the contents. Hand sanitizer, some pretzels, and an airline sticker. I shove everything back in and put it in the back of the seat in front of me. Then, I pull out my headphones. Double-checking to ensure my phone is on airplane mode, I click the shuffle button on my playlist and close my eyes.

It's going to be a long flight, and I've got some thinking to do. The music floats around my head, and I instantly feel calm wash over me.

Images of Tucker penetrate my mind. The way his fingers felt around my throat and how in tune we were together. He knew exactly what I needed before I did. He masterfully made me his in body, mind, and soul.

My heartbeat quickens. I'm not sure if it's because the plane is taking off or if it's because I know where my heart belongs.

Two weeks is a long time. This is going to be the best vacation of my life, despite missing my best friend.

Chapter Fourteen

Lizzy

THEN AGAIN, MAYBE ABSENCE really does make the heart grow fonder . . . especially when it's your childhood best friend who is insanely handsome and you've just discovered how well the two of you fit together.

The captain's voice comes over the speakers. "Ladies and gentlemen, please put away your tray tables and stow your belongings in preparation for landing. We are about twenty minutes away from Venice. We're going in at a warm twenty-two degrees Celsius—that's seventy-two degrees Fahrenheit—and it's nice and sunny, looking like a perfect afternoon. I hope you've had a pleasant flight with us, and we look forward to seeing you again soon. Flight attendants, prepare for landing."

Ding! The seatbelt sign turns on again, and I sigh. That noise is getting on my nerves. My headphones died a couple of hours ago. And, of course, the one thing I forgot to pack was a battery for the portable charger.

I rub my hands over my face and stretch out my right leg as much as I can. With everyone in their seats, it's easier for my leg to be in the aisle without feeling like I'm going to trip someone. There's been a cramp in my leg for the past hour.

How anyone actually enjoys plane rides is beyond me. This sucks.

The wing flaps rumble as the pilot opens them for landing. My stomach does that flip-flop thing it does when you're descending from a certain height. A roller coaster, an elevator, a plane ride.

I close my eyes and take a few deep breaths. A moment later, the wheels hit the tarmac, jostling me in the seat.

Finally.

A flight attendant picks up the intercom to address us. "Thank you for flying with us today. We hope your flight has been enjoyable. Please remain seated while we taxi on the runway and keep your seatbelt on until we make a complete stop at the gate and the seatbelt light is off. Local time is 2:38 p.m. We hope you enjoy your stay here in Venice."

Another flight attendant makes her rounds again, collecting any last-minute trash. I shift in my seat and pull out my phone, switching it off airplane mode. It buzzes with incoming texts from Tucker.

How's the flight going?

Were you able to sleep?

Landed yet?

Text me when you land. That's an order.

I'm aching to respond, but I want to hear his voice the next time we talk, and it's too noisy to make a phone call in the cabin.

Thankfully, people start moving out of first-class and into the jetway, and the rows behind them follow. I grab my backpack, swing it over my shoulder, and follow everyone else into the building.

My bladder is screaming at me again, so I make a beeline to the bathroom. Being one of the first ones off the plane means there's no line for a stall. Within a few minutes, I make my way to the baggage claim area.

Venice International Airport is gorgeous for an airport. Tall windows span one side of the hallway, showing the view of the city. The beauty before me is captivating. It's almost midafternoon, but the sun is still high in the sky against a backdrop of rustic buildings. Interspersed clouds provide some shade over the greenery. I stop for a second to enjoy the view. There's no rush, my luggage will still be waiting for me. Honestly, I'll probably get there before the bags do. It was a big plane.

I can't wait to explore Venice and all it has to offer. Excitement pulses through me for many reasons, and I know I can't wait any longer.

Removing my phone from my back pocket, I unlock it and hover over Tucker's picture. It's now or never.

My finger presses the call icon. It rings once in my ear before he picks up.

"Well, it's about time you called." He laughs.

"I'm in," I say.

His laughter rings out again. "You're in . . . Italy? Good, I'm glad. How was the flight?"

"No, I mean, I'm saying yes."

"Yes to what?"

Without hesitation, I move forward. "Yes to us. Yes to being yours. Yes to all of it."

"Whatever you do, do not scream."

"Huh?" *What's he talking about?*

Before I can utter another word, arms wrap around my waist and I'm spun around. I shriek as my phone flies out of my hand.

"Itching for a punishment already?"

I gasp at the familiar voice. "Tucker? What the hell?"

"Did you really think I'd let you traipse around Italy alone?" He chuckles as he squeezes me against him.

He releases me a second later, and I drop my backpack on the floor and turn to face him.

"Um, *yeah*. You said for me to enjoy my vacation and give you an answer when I got home."

"I lied." He smirks. I swat his arm playfully. "Come here."

He reaches for my neck and pulls me in for a deep kiss, only stopping when a teenager yells, "Get a room!" Laughter falls around us, and I smile against Tucker's lips.

"Let's grab our bags and head to the rental." He grabs my backpack and helps me into it. He also finds my phone a couple of feet away and tosses it in his pocket. Then, he grabs my hand and leads me the rest of the way to baggage claim.

The stroll takes long enough that our three suitcases are the only ones left on the conveyor belt. Tucker lifts them off one at a time and rolls one toward me.

"This one is the heaviest; you can handle it." He flashes me a big smile, and I shake my head, laughing.

"Ever the gentleman." Of course, he handed me the lightest suitcase. Mine were both pretty heavy, but shoes and toiletries are lighter than clothes.

A minute later, we're walking up to the rental counter.

"Ciao, come potrei aiutarti?" *Hello, how may I help you?*

"Sì, we have a reservation under Carter, Elizabeth."

"Un momento, per favore." She taps away on the keyboard and frowns. "I don't have a reservation under that name. Is there another one, perhaps?"

"Try Banks, Tucker." He hands the woman his license and passport.

"Ah, sì, here it is." The agent enters his information, and the printer whirs as it prints the rental agreement.

She sets the papers on the counter. "Sign here, here, and here, please." While he signs the dotted lines, she places the receipt and a key next to him. "The car is in the lot. If this doesn't suit you, you can trade the key in with the attendant outside. We have three other cars ready to go, il signore."

Tucker turns to me. "You ready, Sunshine?" He swipes the keys off the counter.

My grin is bigger than ever. "Always."

Chapter Fifteen

Tucker

THE KEY IS TO a tiny green car, and Lizzy is not thrilled. Instead, she picks a blue convertible GTS 311 Gigi, and it's so gorgeous. It's a perfect fit for us. We meet with the attendant and switch the keys.

I open the passenger door for her, and she gapes at me.

"Were you planning on driving?"

A bemused look flashes across her face.

Groaning, I tell her, "I'm so glad you didn't come here alone. You'd drive on the wrong side of the road and crash!"

Uncontrollable laughter bubbles out of her because she knows I'm right. She rounds the car and climbs in.

Quickly, I shove the luggage into the trunk and come back to the driver's side of the car. I hit the button to move the top back, climb in, and adjust the seat. At six foot three inches tall, I need all the room I can get.

Meanwhile, Lizzy is five foot six, and the seats hug her perfectly. Her auburn hair is now up in a messy bun, and she looks adorable as she takes in her surroundings. There's a twinkle in her eyes, and she shines like the sun. If I wasn't already in love with her, this would be the moment I'd fall. She looks so calm and serene, as if she belongs here. A smile tugs at her mouth, and she glances over at me.

"Well, what are you waiting for?" Her tongue slips out to lick her plump lips.

I pull up the hotel on my phone and plug the coordinates into the car navigation system. "Hold on tight, baby."

The tires squeal as we pull out of the parking lot, marking the beginning of our Italy vacation.

This whole trip is about Lizzy, and I cannot wait to shower her with the love and attention she deserves. I reach over and squeeze her thigh with my left hand.

She places her hand under mine and entwines our fingers, gently squeezing my hand in return.

There's a look of pure enjoyment on her face.

Lizzy pulls out her phone, and it's like she's reading my mind. She leans against me and yells over the wind, "Smile!"

I tilt my head toward her and flash a smile. She takes a few pictures, then looks at them. Once she's satisfied, she leans into me again and kisses my cheek.

Instead of driving the most direct route, we're taking the scenic route. There's nothing like the countryside in Italy. Tons of hills covered with grass and flowers, little cottages here and there. It's peaceful. I've never seen anything like it.

Her hand snakes up my thigh, inching closer to my cock. She's looking out her window, pretending nothing's happening. With just a simple touch, I'm primed, ready to pounce, and it takes every ounce of willpower I have to not pull the car over. Now, she's tracing her fingers up and down my thigh and barely grazing my erection.

I growl a warning. "Lizzy."

Still looking out into the fields, she grabs my length through my pants and gives it a small squeeze. I know she heard me because her head tilts slightly toward me. Her finger teasingly traces the outline of my hard cock. Then she stops and puts her hand on my thigh again.

We continue driving for a moment before her hand moves back up to my groin.

She's playing with fire, not knowing she's about to get burned. There's nothing around us but fields, and we haven't seen another person in a good ten minutes or so.

Slowly, I let off the gas, and the car comes to a stop off the side of the road.

It's only then that she looks at me. "What's wrong?" she asks.

"You're a tease." I smirk. "It's about time you do something about it." I unbutton my jeans and lower the zipper while looking around us.

Keeping her eyes on me, she wets her bottom lip. I pull my cock out and grab the base, then tug my hand up and back down.

"See, this is what you do to me. You have three—" She cuts me off by leaning over me and taking the tip of my cock in her mouth. She sucks gently, and I groan. "Fuuuuck."

Her mouth opens wider, and my shaft disappears. I've had blow jobs before, but there's that deep sense of euphoria when it's with someone you've wanted for so long. Lizzy tongues the underside of the head, and my hips buck. I close my eyes and bask in the feeling of her mouth around my cock. When she sucks the tip again, adding a little more pressure, I thread my fingers through her messy hair and guide her head down. Then, I fist her hair and pull her head back up. Her jaw tightens, and she moans, adding a new sensation.

Before she can stop it, I fuck her mouth by thrusting my hips as I hold her head in place. My cock hits the back of her throat, and she allows me to slip down. I moan and pull her head up before she gags. She looks up at me with teary eyes, my cock still in her mouth.

"You are so beautiful." I wipe a thumb under her eye to catch a tear. "Unless you want me to come inside your pretty mouth and down your throat, you need to get out of this car and put your hands on the hood."

Her mouth slides off my cock, leaving a trail of saliva connecting us. With a satisfied smile, she wipes her mouth with the back of her hand before speaking.

"As you wish, Sir." She climbs out of the car and faces the windshield, sets her palms down on the hood, and locks eyes with me. Lust drips in the silence between us.

I open my door, step out, and walk over to her. Once I'm behind her, I wrap one arm around her waist and force her chest down onto the car. She adjusts her hands so they're closer to her face and more comfortable.

"Hmm, the sweet and dirty things I want to do to you." I let the unspoken words hang in the air as I run my hands down her body.

She shivers when I make it to her waist and wiggles her ass against me. I reach around to unbutton her jeans, and her breath hitches as I lower my hand inside. I caress her mound, then dip my finger inside her underwear.

"You're soaking already, Sunshine."

She answers with a moan that turns into a whine of protest when I remove my hand. Grabbing the waist of her jeans, I tug them down to her knees, taking her thong with it. My hand comes down on her ass with a loud crack, and she gasps.

I rub the area, and then spank her again. Her ass wiggles, but a small moan slips past her lips. My hand hits her ass one more time, and I appreciate the red handprints—*my* handprints—left on her rear. I slip my hand in between her legs and find her sweet hole. I'm only cupping her pussy, barely touching her, when I hear something behind me.

A car.

Lizzy stills. I shift my body to cover her, but before the car reaches us, it turns down a different road.

I move my fingers between her lips, feeling the wetness trickle down my hand as I push my fingers inside her.

"My, my. You should have told me you were an exhibitionist . . . This could make things really interesting."

Her breathy moan tells me I'm right. I lean over her and kiss her neck as I whisper, "As much as I want to fuck you right now, I need to taste you. Put one knee on the hood of the car, and then stay right where you are."

I withdraw my fingers, and give her room to step out of her pants. Then I sit on the ground, positioning myself in front of her but between her legs. My back hits something on the car, but it doesn't bother me. There's other things on my mind.

Her glistening pussy is right in front of my face. Damn, she smells so sweet. I flick my tongue out to taste her sweetness and reach out to grab her ass with both hands. When her ass is firmly in my grip, I tilt her hips so I can line myself up, and I begin my assault on her clit.

She starts to writhe on top of me, moaning. Her moans seem incredibly loud in the otherwise silent field. "Oh, fuck!"

I move my tongue down to her opening and continue my assault, licking every drop of her wetness. I groan and loosen my grip on her ass. Moving back to her clit, I suck on the bud and push a finger inside her pussy, then another.

"Tucker . . ." She grinds on my face, chasing her orgasm. She's so close.

I suck hard on her clit and pump my fingers. Her pussy tightens, and I'm rewarded with her orgasm. The first one, that is.

After a few moments, I stand up and watch her beautifully spent body rest on the hood of the car.

With a devious grin on my face, I squat down to meet her gaze. "You didn't ask permission to come." I shake my head.

In between pants, she answers me with a sly smile. "Not. My. Fault."

I kiss her forehead lightly and move behind her, pull out my cock, and line myself up with her entrance. She hasn't fully recovered from her orgasm when I thrust into her, and her pussy sucks me in deep.

"Fuuuuck, you're so tight." I groan and thrust again, then pull almost all the way out before thrusting back in. Reaching down between her legs, I pinch her clit between my fingers. She's so wet.

Her moans fill the air, but it's not what I need. I need to see her fall apart. Slowly, I slide out of her. "Turn around."

She turns to face me with a questioning look in her eyes. Before she can say anything, I grab her waist and set her down on the hood. I move in between her legs but don't thrust into her. Instead, I tilt my head down and kiss her. She moans into my mouth, and only then do I thrust into her. Hard. Frenzied.

Her legs wrap around me, and I pull her ass closer to me, not letting her go.

I break our kiss to trail kisses down her neck. "I want to see how pretty you are when you come, Lizzy. Touch yourself and scream my name as you come for me."

Her hand snakes in between us and she strums her clit. My movements slow down so I can let her lead and enjoy the view as I watch her get herself off on my cock. She flicks her clit back and forth while her hips make small rotations, and she throws her head back on a loud moan.

"Oh," she breathes.

"That's it, baby." I look down between her legs and watch her slick pussy suck my cock inside her. The sight alone is enough to make me come. "Come for me, Lizzy."

Her fingers move a little faster, her hips thrust to meet mine, and she wraps her other arm around my neck. "Kiss me," she whispers.

I'd do anything for her. My lips crash against hers, and her pussy contracts around my cock. A split second later, she's coming hard, breaking our kiss to scream her release.

I open my eyes and see nothing but ecstasy across her features. She looks so goddamn beautiful. As I take back over thrusting, my cock twitches, and I'm done for. I'm lost in the moment. I'm lost in the pleasure. And I'm lost in what is finally mine. I shatter.

Moments later, her giggles pull me out of my trance. "You okay?"

"Yeah, baby. I'm perfect." I pull out of her and tuck myself back into my pants. "Let's get you dressed and back into the car. We still have tons of adventure left."

She rolls her eyes. "Well, duh. I know you didn't take me to Italy just to have sex with me on the side of the road." She hops off the car and bends over to pick up her thong and pants.

I groan. "Keep that up and we'll never make it to the hotel."

"Keep what up?" She bats her eyes innocently.

She's anything but innocent.

After she's fully dressed, I open the door for her and help her into the car.

"Such a gentleman." She winks at me.

"Being a gentleman doesn't at all mean I won't hesitate to tie you up, pin you down, spank your ass, bite you, or pull your hair." I wink back and close her door, then jog around the car and climb into the driver's side.

As soon as we buckle up, Lizzy reaches over and turns on the radio. Somehow, she manages to find the only English station, which happens to be country music. The wind blows through her hair as she sings along with the radio.

She always sings a little off-key, but that's what makes it better. She doesn't need to be perfect, and she doesn't try to be.

I grab Lizzy's hand and bring it up to my mouth. Kissing the back of her hand, I lace my fingers through hers.

Thirty miles left to the hotel, and I can't think of a better way to spend the next two weeks.

Chapter Sixteen

Two years later...

Voices chatter through the room while my coworkers and I wait for Melanie to start the presentation. Our small accounting firm has acquired a new office in Colorado, and we're waiting for Melanie to break the news whether she's staying, or who will take her place if she leaves.

I'm looking over the numbers on the profit and loss statement in front of me when the room falls quiet. I glance up to see Melanie waltz into in the room.

"Good morning, everyone! We have a lot to cover in this meeting, so let's get right to it. Lizzy, why don't you start us off?" She nods in my direction.

"Sure." I stand up and address my boss and coworkers. "Slaw Daddy's and Jamba Juice both had a great second quarter. Joe's Steakhouse came in a little low, but that's to be expected after the holidays. All is shaping up nicely going into Q3."

"That's wonderful, glad to hear it. Next?"

I sit down and tune out Jack as he drones on about how well his clients are doing. Usually, I pay close attention to these meetings in case something comes up and I need to cover for the accountant. Sorry, Jack. It's not my fault Saturday night's sexcapades are invading my thoughts today.

Tucker has been testing my limits. Some of it is hard. Really hard. Almost-using-the-safeword hard.

My body has been bent in ways I never thought possible. Being with Tucker has unearthed a dozen kinks I didn't know about myself. Saturday night was the toughest session we've had.

Ever since we got back from Italy, when he discovered I enjoy people watching me in ways they shouldn't, he's been dragging me to the masked club . . . a sex club.

Crimson is so hush-hush about it. No one actually knows the name of the club or who the owner is. It's simply an establishment that exists by word of mouth, but you have to know someone who knows someone to get in.

There are many rules for a patron to abide by to make it a safe and consensual environment for all.

Saturday night, Tucker wanted to try something new—a thrusting dildo sex machine. I've played with toys before, but they were always something I could control.

A sex toy that would fuck me into oblivion? Intriguing, but definitely out of my comfort zone. Turns out, out of the comfort zone is where the best experiences come from.

My mind flashes back to Saturday night.

The masked club had over a dozen playrooms—some for watching, others for playing—along with a couple of rooms that were completely secluded. Tucker led us into a secluded area and ordered me to undress.

Wearing nothing but a mask and my favorite red lace bra, Tucker strapped me into a chair that resembled one of the tables in a doctor's office. Except the bottom half was missing, and instead of laying down, I was sitting upright. There was hardly any room for my ass without sliding off. I guess that's why the stirrups were there. Thankfully, the owner had dressed them up so they didn't look so cold and doctor-ish.

He quickly tied my feet up, then moved to drag the machine closer to me. My whole lower body was vulnerable, my holes exposed. I was completely at his mercy.

Tucker opened and closed a few drawers, grabbed a couple of items from behind the machine, and then turned it on.

My body shivered in anticipation when I heard the low rumble of the machine.

"Small, medium, or big?" he asked as he held up three dildos for me to choose from.

"Small, please."

He laughed. "Medium it is." His voice commanding.

"Yes, Sir." I nodded and watched him skillfully maneuver the dildo onto the machine's plate. Then he grabbed a bottle of lube and squirted some into his hand.

His hand stroked the dildo. *Fuck, that was hot.* "Tucker?" He looked up at me. "I need you," I whispered.

A wicked grin crossed his face. "Soon." He turned his attention back to the dildo. Once it was fully coated with lube, he flipped the first switch on the left.

The arm of the machine extended toward me, and the dildo barely touched my exposed clit. My body jolted at the contact, and the arm pulled back. Tucker pushed the machine another inch closer to me. The tip of the dildo fully touched my clit, but not enough.

Tucker adjusted the machine again, and then flipped the second switch. The arm started moving faster. This time, it made contact with my pussy, but without entering me. A groan fell from my lips.

"So beautiful." He smiled at me and flipped the third switch, halting the machine's movements. Stepping around the machine, he placed a hand on my ankle and trailed his fingers up my leg as he approached my head.

His fingers sent shocks through my body as his hand made its way to my center.

He dipped a finger into my pussy and pulled it out, then trailed the wetness up to my stomach. "Mmm, so wet." He cupped one breast in his hand and leaned in to whisper in my ear. "Pretend they're watching your pussy while you get fucked hard by this dildo. You'll be screaming my name in three minutes."

His lips captured mine in a forceful kiss, and I reached up to thread my fingers through his hair.

I was lost in my surroundings when the dildo slid into me, quickly and with little resistance. "Ahh!" I cried out against Tucker's lips.

Holy mother of god.

Tucker deepened the kiss, savoring my taste with his tongue. I moaned into his mouth as the dildo pulled all the way out and shoved back into me.

It moved slowly—in and out, in and out. After a couple of thrusts, it started moving faster. Tucker swallowed my moans. Something clattered on the ground behind me, but I couldn't turn to look. Without breaking our kiss, Tucker's grasp on my breast became sharper, and he brought his other hand to my throat and applied a small amount of pressure. The dildo moved at the same pace, pumping in and out of my pussy.

A second later, the pace picked up a notch and it pumped inside me faster. I broke our kiss, the need to scream too much. My moans filled the room. I couldn't stop, even if I wanted to. "Please?" I looked for Tucker's approval as I gripped the armrests on the chair so hard my knuckles turned white.

He nodded, and his grip on my throat tightened as he moved his other hand down to my clit. The second he pinched my clit between his fingers, I came undone, screaming his name, just like he said I would.

Fuuuuuck. He released my throat but didn't stop touching me.

"I'm so proud of you," he murmured, sending shivers down my spine.

The orgasm racked through my body, so intense I couldn't speak. My juices leaked out of me every time the dildo retracted. His fingers still pinched my clit hard, and he trailed kisses from my neck down to my breasts. He pulled one side of my bra down, exposing my puckered nipple.

"Please," I whimpered.

His eyes darkened as he smirked. "Please what?"

"Please. Come," I said between breaths. My muscles were tensing, my skin sensitive to the touch.

Instead of answering me, Tucker licked the area around my breast, down my cleavage, and back up to my nipple. He flicked his tongue against my nipple, then took it between his teeth and bit down.

"Oh, god." A moan rolled through my body when he released my nipple.

The dildo was still thrusting in and out of my swollen pussy, Tucker still pinching my clit. "Just like that, baby. You're doing so good. Come again for me."

He bit down on my nipple and released my clit. The sudden movement of both happening at the same time sent my body into overdrive.

I fill the room with loud moans as I came.

Tucker's voice filled my ears. "That's it. Take it, baby." The dildo continued its assault, and my orgasm didn't stop.

After a long minute, my orgasm subsided, and sobs racked my body.

"You good, Sunshine?"

I struggled to take a deep breath and nod, trying to concentrate on my breathing. I barely registered Tucker turning off the machine and untying me. He scooped me up into his arms and carried me to the bathroom, where he started a warm bath.

"Excuse me, is there a Lizzy in here?"

Hearing my name jolts me out of my daydream. I squeeze my thighs together and blink a few times before I realize I'm still in the office.

"Uh, yes, that's me." I raise my hand.

A delivery man walks toward me and hands me a package. "Special delivery."

"Thanks." I grab the package. "Sorry, guys. Please continue."

Melanie is the first to jump in. "Oooh, what's in the package?"

"What's in the box?" someone says after her, followed by a few laughs.

I chuckle and reach for the gold card on top of the package. I carefully remove it and open the card to find a set of instructions.

Let's go on an adventure. The rules are simple. Follow the directions on the back of the card and get your next clue.

Melanie appears over my shoulder, and I quickly clutch the card against my chest. "What's on the back of the card?"

"Oh! Don't sneak up on people like that." I try to wave her away. "Let's finish up the meeting, guys."

She rolls her eyes. "Fine, have it your way. Does anyone have anything else to add?"

Everyone shakes their heads.

"All right, meeting adjourned." Jack is the first out of the door, almost. "Ahem, before you leave . . . I'll be heading up the new office in Colorado, and Jack will be taking my place as lead manager."

Cheers erupt throughout the conference room and a few coworkers give Jack high-fives, while others tell Melanie they'll miss her. I'm in the latter camp—not that I'm not happy for Jack. I am, and between Melanie and me, I was her first pick to head up the Colorado office. I politely declined because a move isn't what I had in mind, and I'm not ready for the extra work at the moment. If she would've asked me two years ago, sure. But now, it feels like Tucker and I are just beginning. Besides, I can't leave the spot where we laid my mom to rest.

Although I'm disappointed she didn't choose me as her successor, I understand it. In a way, I turned down the promotion when I turned down her offer. For now, I'm happy where I am.

After congratulating Jack, I gather up the papers in front of me and head back into my office. As soon as I'm behind my desk, I take out the card and read the back.

Unbutton your blouse and take a selfie. Show me your bra and your beautiful eyes. You have thirty minutes. One second late and face punishment.

A blush creeps up my face. *What is he up to now?* I stand up and head to the bathroom, leaving the package on my desk.

Me: (Incoming Picture)

Tucker: You look so sexy.

Me: Thank you, Sir.

Tucker: Fuck, your tits drive me wild.

Tucker: Did you open the package yet?

Me: Not yet. It was delivered in the middle of a meeting.

Tucker: Open it and put it on before you leave. Take a picture showing me you have it on, and then I'll give you the next clue.

Me: Yes, Sir.

I button up my blouse, straighten the rest of my clothes, and head back into my office.

The rest of the day goes by pretty quickly. Thankfully, it's the beginning of the month, so there's not too much piled on my desk. Other than the package. It's been taunting me all day.

It's close enough to the end of the day, so I tear open the box to reveal a small butt plug and a tiny bottle of lube.

"What the . . . Oh, Tucker." I shake my head and gather my things. Stuffing the package in my purse, I close the office door behind me and head for the bathroom to do something naughty for the second time today.

Chapter Seventeen

ME: Do you know how difficult it is to take a picture of this thing?

Me: (Incoming Picture)

Tucker: Good girl.

Me: My next clue?

Tucker: So sassy :p

Me: Please, Sir?

Tucker: I need you to do a few things first.

Tucker: Pick up my dry cleaning, then go to the bakery and pick up some brownies. I already put in the order.

Me: And then?

Tucker: Do not remove the plug.

Me: The clue?

I shove the phone into my pocket and walk a few steps to the sink. *Oh, fuck.* The couple of times I've had something in my ass, Tucker was right there next to me, and I wasn't walking anywhere. *This feels weird.*

Walking quickly out of the building, I thank my lucky stars there's no one around for me to talk to. When I make it to my car, I throw everything onto the passenger seat and pull out my phone.

No new messages.

The jerk leaves me on read.

I shift in my seat and groan. A shot of pleasure rips through my body as I roll my hips forward. *Dammit.* He loves to tease me.

A couple of minutes later, I arrive at the dry cleaners. I roll my hips a couple more times. *Okay, I didn't think I'd like this, but it feels good.* My pussy grows slick, and I clench my thighs together.

I take a deep breath, then get out of the car and walk to the dry cleaners. Thankfully, the cashier doesn't want to make small talk today, and I'm out in less than five minutes. I barely make it out without moaning.

Fuck, I'm so turned on. There's a thrill in knowing I'm doing something naughty where no one knows.

The bakery is a couple of blocks away, so it takes me a minute to get there. Annie sees me pull up and waves to me from inside the door. I wave back to her and climb out of the car.

As I rush inside, another jolt of pleasure shoots through me, and I shiver.

"Are you all right?" Annie asks.

"Absolutely." *Not. My ass is on fire, and I want to fuck my boyfriend to hell and back.* I take a breath. "A dozen brownies, please."

"Coming right up!" She disappears behind the door marked Employees Only and comes back a moment later. "Here you go."

The pink box is tied with a bow, and another gold card is peeking out from underneath the ribbon.

"Thank you! Put it on Tucker's tab, please."

"You got it," Annie says with a smile.

"Have a good night!" I call out before rushing back to my car.

I'm panting with need when I open the card.

Go to where we first started. Strip down to nothing except your heels and the plug. Wait for me patiently and you will be rewarded.

A heat fills me, warming my core. As if I'd go anywhere other than home—after all, it is my favorite place to be.

Not long after we got back from Italy, we started renovating the house my mom left me. Tucker worked his magic with contacts from work, and they turned the abandoned house into my perfect home. It took months of planning and resulted in a few arguments between Tucker and me, but everything finally came together six months ago.

Since then, Tucker has moved in with me and has made it his mission to fuck me on every single surface he can. Relentlessly.

I pull into the driveway in record time and see his car sitting there.

Shit.

Chapter Eighteen

Tucker

"YOU'RE LATE."

She comes rushing through the door and sets the brownies on the entryway table. "I know, I'm sorry."

"Come here and kneel." I'm leaning against the counter in the kitchen, still dressed in my suit.

Lizzy scurries into the kitchen and kneels before me, head dipped into her chest.

"You're late," I say again.

"Sorry, Sir. It won't happen again."

We both know it will. "Look at me, Sunshine."

Her head lifts up to meet my gaze. I see the lust swirling in her sweet eyes. She needs someone who sees the fire in her eyes and wants to play with it.

"You look stunning on your knees. Your pretty plump lips are waiting to be kissed, but they'll look much better around my cock." I unbuckle my belt and motion for her to do the rest.

She doesn't waste any time freeing me. A drop of pre-cum glistens on my tip, and she swirls it around the head with her thumb, eliciting a groan from me. Her tongue darts out and licks up and down my shaft, then she takes me in her mouth and looks up at me.

Goddamn. The sight alone makes me want to come. I'll never tire of the picture before me. I smirk and bring my hand around to the back of her head. She continues to suck me. I let her set the pace for a minute. When I can't take it anymore, I shove her head down and feel her gag against me.

Keeping her head in place, I fuck her pretty mouth. The sound of her gags and my moans fill the room. Soon, the familiar twitch pulls at my cock, and I release a long groan as I come down her throat. She moans against me, swallowing every last drop, then pulls off me and licks her lips.

"Thank you, Sir."

I tuck myself back in my pants before answering. "Strip. Leave only your heels and the plug. Time for your punishment." I extend my hand down to help her get up.

She nods and takes my hand. Facing me, she slowly unbuttons her blouse and lets it fall to the ground. She does the same with her bra, then steps out of her pants and makes her way over to the couch in front of the fireplace.

"Aren't you forgetting something?"

A pair of lace panties hit the floor in front of me. I pick them up and bring them to my face. Inhaling her sweet scent, I stifle a groan.

I pull my belt out of the loops and crack it in the silence. She jiggles her ass in response. As I round the couch, I admire her naked form. Her chest rises and falls with her ragged breaths. My fingers trail down her back, and she lifts her ass up, silently begging.

Without warning, I bring the belt down on her fleshy bottom. "Ahh!" she cries out, but she arches her back for more.

Another crack of the belt rings out as it strikes her skin, and my hand moves to caress the now-red lines across her rear. I pause to rub the sting before I do it again.

"Please," she whimpers.

Crack!

"Oh, fuck." Her body shakes.

After I caress her again, I move my fingers up to find her pussy slick with desire. I dip two fingers in, and she lets out a moan of relief.

"Ooooh."

My other hand moves to the plug sitting in her ass. I barely touch the end, and she shrieks.

"Hmm, Lizzy. Look how responsive you are." My fingers move in and out of her pussy, and I grab the base of the plug this time and tilt it up. A long moan falls from her lips. I tilt the base down and can feel it through her pussy. Then I slowly pull the plug out as I move my fingers faster. She's thrusting her hips back into me, fucking herself on my fingers and the plug. I push it back in and pull it out again, and she pants.

"Oh, god. Tucker, don't stop." I lean down and leave a kiss on her ass cheek, then bite it.

Her pussy contracts against my fingers, sucking them in deeper.

"You're a dirty girl, Lizzy. Your tight cunt is dripping."

She's right there on the edge, waiting for me to say the words she needs to hear. I continue to work the plug and my fingers together.

"Come for me," I say.

And she falls.

"Yes! Tucker, yes!" She screams my name as she comes, and her body goes slack against the back of the couch as she breathes heavily.

I remove the plug and set it on the coffee table next to me. My fingers are still pumping inside her, her juices covering my hand. I add a third finger. *She's so perfect.* I reach my other hand around her to between her legs and graze her clit.

The contact jolts her body. "Oh, god."

"You can take it, baby. You'll come for me again."

"No, no." She mutters. "Too much."

"What was that?"

"I can't, sir. Not again," she says in between shallow breaths.

My fingers move faster inside her pussy. Her loud moans soon fill the room again.

"Mmm, that's it. Take what I give you, my beautiful girl." I toy with her clit and pinch it—just the way she likes it.

She screams as her orgasm comes crashing through her body once more. When her breathing starts to even out, I remove my fingers and grab her waist, pulling her close to me. I move us down on the couch and wrap my arms around her, letting her rest.

Her fingers trail up and down my arm. "Mmm, Tucker?"

"Yes, Sunshine?"

"You set me up, didn't you?" She giggles.

"I don't know what you're talking about." I grin behind her head.

"Oh, hush." She laces her fingers through mine and squeezes. "You've got me all figured out."

I kiss her head. "Mmm."

"I love you."

"Not more than I love you." She snuggles closer.

These past two years have been amazing. I know she's had her moments where she was sure we wouldn't be together. Silly girl.

Safe to say, now she's in my arms, I am never letting her go. The next hunt is already underway. There's one thing left to do.

And she won't be happy when she finds out.

Fuck it.

Chapter Nineteen

ONE WEEK LATER...

"Ma'am, line one is holding for you." The new temp peeks her head in and motions to my phone.

I look up. "Thank you, Jess."

Cradling the phone between my shoulder and my ear, I press the flashing button. "Hello, Lizzy speaking." My eyes flicker across the computer screen at the email before me.

"Hello. I'm calling from Crimson Senior Living Center. It seems your dad has had a stumble in the shower, and he's asking for you."

My body freezes.

I haven't seen my father in a little over a year. Not by choice, either, but after our last encounter, I would have stayed away anyway. The last time I saw him, he had an outburst and threw a chair at me, yelling obscenities and spitting out it was my fault my mom died. Not that I believed him, but it hurt nonetheless.

The center advised it might be better not to come in, as seeing me only upsets him. They were crazy to assume I'd want to come back after that. I shake my head to ward off the memory.

"Ma'am?"

Her voice startles me. "Uh, yes. I can stop by later today." *Why is he asking for me?* The question is on the tip of my tongue, but I decide against it.

"Yes, ma'am, thank you." She hangs up.

My mind is anywhere but at work. I run a hand through my hair and glance at the clock. The center called around nine o'clock. It's now a little after noon. I'm not going to get anything else done today. "Hey, Jess?" I call out.

Her dainty figure appears in my doorway. "Yes, ma'am?" She smiles.

"I'm taking the rest of the day off due to a personal matter. Please reschedule the rest of my meetings."

"Will do, ma'am."

"One more thing," I call out to her before she retreats back to her desk. "You can stop calling me ma'am. Elizabeth is fine."

"Thank you." She nods, then leaves.

Quickly, I gather my things and walk to my car. When I climb in, I turn the air conditioner to its lowest setting and roll down the windows. It's hotter than is typical for early fall. Once the air has cooled down, I turn it on full blast and enjoy the cold air running through my hair. I turn on the radio to drown out my thoughts, although the music is never quite loud enough.

All too quickly, I pull into the parking lot of the center and find a spot close to the door, turn off the car, and reluctantly walk inside to the receptionist's desk.

"Hi, welcome to Crimson Senior Living Center. How may I help you?"

"Hi. I'm here to see my father, Roger Carter?"

"You must be Lizzy." She reaches out to shake my hand, and I give her a small smile as I shake hers.

"I am."

She nods. "Please sign in and be sure to sign out when you leave. He's in the common area. I trust you know the way?"

I nod and, after signing in, take a few steps down the hall to my right. There's a small knot in my throat, which I try to gulp down. After a couple of deep breaths, I cautiously make my way down the hall.

There is no good time to see my father. Yet, here he is, dressed in a long robe, his hair unkempt, and in the slippers that have worn down to nothing. The only thing different about him is that his skin has more of a yellow tint than it did last time.

As I walk up to him, I clear my throat. "Hello, Roger."

"Oh, Lizzy! I'm glad you came!" He rises from his seat and reaches for me, and I let him draw me into a hug, then I quickly pull away.

"They said you were asking for me. Are you doing okay?" I ask.

"The better question is, what are you doing with a boy like Tucker?" He raises his voice, waving a hand in front of his face. "I'm fine. It was a small slip in the shower. Nothing major."

I flinch, taking a step back. "A boy like Tucker?"

He points his finger at me. "He's no good for you. I've always told you that."

"We're not here to talk about the men in my life." I blink furiously as my hands clench into fists by my side. "How do you even know about him?"

Roger's lip curls in disgust. "He came to see me." His chest juts out and he lifts his chin, leaning back in his seat. "He didn't tell you about that, did he?"

I feel the color drain from my face, and I bite my lip.

"He shouldn't have done that." Bile rises in my throat.

"I told him to stay away from you."

"S-stay away from me? Don't start acting like you care now." My hands tremble. My heart races. *Why the hell would Tucker come to see my father? He knows how I feel about him.* I shake my head.

My father starts to speak, but I hold my hand up. "No, we're done." Heat crawls up my body as the roar in my ears becomes louder, and I take a deep breath.

"I'm not like you, Roger," I bite out. "I have people that care about me, that love me. So listen closely when I say *I don't need you.*"

With that, I turn around, but he reaches out and grasps my wrist, pulling me back.

"You listen here, you ungrateful little bitch. You will be nothing to him. He'll leave you too, just like your momma did." His voice drips with venom.

I snatch my arm out of his grip and walk down the hall, scribble my name on the sign-out form, and rush outside.

"Ahhh!" I scream into the air as I kick the trashcan on the sidewalk. A few people look in my direction, but I don't care.

The next few minutes are a blur. Only two things I know for certain. One: I step on the gas and speed my way through town. And two: All I see is red as I do so.

Chapter Twenty

Tucker

THE FRONT DOOR SLAMS, rattling the windows beside me and pulling me out of the story. I pick up my phone to check the time. It's the middle of the day. *She shouldn't be home for another few hours.*

Before I can get out of the chair in the library to greet her, another door slams shut, shaking the bones of the old house.

Oh, so that's how you want to play today? Game on.

I give her a second before I close my book and stalk toward the bedroom. When I open the door and peer in, she's pacing between the bathroom and the closet. She's muttering and hasn't noticed me yet.

The moment her back is turned, I pounce. My fingers weave through her hair, then grip the hair at her nape. I spin her around to face me and slam her body against the wall.

"Oof!" The force of my body against hers pushes the air from her lungs.

"Is that any way to greet me?" I flash her a wicked smile before claiming her mouth in a kiss.

Her lips part, granting me access. I slip my tongue into her mouth and deepen our kiss. She inhales my scent and hooks her arms around my neck.

Fuck, this woman. My cock aches for her, and we've barely begun.

Closing the minimal distance between us, I grind my hips against her. She lets out a breathy moan.

"Please," she whimpers. "Use me."

I can't hide the grin on my face. *One of my favorite phrases.* My thumb grazes her bottom lip, then trails down until my hand reaches her throat and grips tightly. We stumble from the bedroom into the bathroom, and before I bend her over the counter, I rip her blouse off. Buttons scatter all over the floor. "You won't be needing this anymore."

Next to go is her knee-length skirt. In one swift motion, I pull it down, revealing a black thong. I groan in appreciation and rub her ass, then bring my hand down in a loud smack.

"Ahh!"

I smack her ass again and rub the sore area, then dip my fingers into her pussy. "Look at you already. Soaking wet." Lazily, I pump my fingers a few times before withdrawing them.

Lizzy whines and jiggles her ass. The smack echoes off the walls as I lay another one on her reddening ass.

"Fuck, baby girl."

The next smack is harder than she expects, and her head grazes the wall. I lean over her body, grinding my cock against her ass, and whisper in her ear. "You are so pretty like this. Bent over, ass up, your needy cunt exposed. Such a dirty little slut . . ."

She's panting underneath me, and her eyes flutter closed.

My hand comes down again, and her whole body jerks.

"More," she breathes.

I oblige, doing it again and again.

Her breaths come out in sobs, and the whisper is so low and quiet, I almost miss it.

"Skittles."

My body freezes, and it takes a second for my brain to catch up. A split second later, I turn and draw her into a hug as I kiss the top of her head.

This is the first time she's used the safeword. Ever.

"What's wrong, Sunshine?"

Tears flow down her face, and she wraps her arms around me even tighter.

I walk us over to the bed and lie down. Her body shakes with each sob that passes through her, and my heart breaks. I smooth her hair while we wait.

"Shh, it's okay. I'm here."

A few minutes pass before she speaks. "Don't leave me."

"Look at me, Lizzy." She tilts her head up to meet my eyes. "You never have to worry about that. I'm not going anywhere."

She nods but doesn't say anything else. I give her another minute before I say, "Is everything okay?"

"No." Lizzy shakes her head. "I saw Roger today."

Shit. I inhale sharply and wait for her to continue.

"He's sick." She sniffs.

"I know."

"No, he's *sick*. Demented and vile." She moves to sit up. "He said you went to see him?"

I nod and sit up with her against the headboard. "Yes, I did."

Hurt flashes through her eyes. "Why didn't you tell me?"

"I . . . It was supposed to be a surprise."

She raises her eyebrows. "A surprise?"

"What did Roger say?"

"That you're not good for me." Her voice trembles. "That I'm nothing, and you'll leave me just like my mom did."

"Oh, Lizzy." I pull her into a hug. "Why did you go see him?"

"One of the nurses called and said he fell in the shower. I guess he was asking for me." She sighs. "I hadn't seen him in a year, so I figured I needed to go."

"Is he okay?"

She scoffs. "Oh, he's just fine, not that it matters. I told him we were done and I wasn't coming back."

"Ah, there's my good girl." A small smile appears on her face. "Are you hungry? Let's get you something to eat." I twist away and get out of bed.

"Yes, Sir." She giggles as she wipes the tears from her eyes. "And, Tucker? I'm sorry."

I turn back to face her. "You have absolutely nothing to be sorry about, Lizzy." I kiss her sweet lips. "Never be sorry about using the safeword. Now, get dressed and come help me with the food."

She rolls her eyes but gets out of bed, grabs a cute pair of sleep shorts, and heads into the bathroom.

A few minutes later, she emerges and wraps her arms around my waist from behind. The spatula clatters on the counter when I spin around to face her.

"You okay?" I ask her.

"I won't be if you burn those pancakes." She laughs and reaches around me to rescue them, flipping two over and checking the others. "Pancakes are the best comfort food. How did I get so lucky?"

"Nah, I'm the lucky one." I wrap my arms around her and inhale her scent. "You are the sunshine to any darkness. Don't let anyone dim your light, especially him."

Her body relaxes against mine, and happiness fills me, despite Roger's attempt to destroy our relationship.

He treats me with disgust—always has—and while I knew I shouldn't have gone to see him, I can't finish the scavenger hunt without him.

Chapter Twenty-One

Two weeks later . . .

There's still one thing that bugs me about my encounter with Roger. Why did Tucker go see him? He would've needed a good reason to, and I've been racking my brain trying to find one.

Neither of us has brought up my father since then.

"Hello . . . Earth to Lizzy." Moxie waves a hand in front of my face.

"Huh?" I shake my head.

"Where'd you go?" Julie asks, coming back from the kitchen with our drinks.

"Oh." I pause. "It's still bugging me."

"Just let it go. I'm sure Tucker had his reasons." Moxie takes one of the cups from Julie and takes a sip.

"You'll only drive yourself crazy," Julie agrees.

"Okay, y'all are supposed to be my friends, not his." I laugh as I take the cup from Julie's outstretched hand.

A girls' night is exactly what I need. It's been a long week for all of us. The Twilight Club has been expanded and the restaurant opened—work's busier than ever for Moxie. It's inventory week at the bookstore for Julie. And, for me, it's a big adjustment with Jack in charge now that Melanie is officially in Colorado. Besides, Tucker is away at a conference for the weekend, so it's the perfect time for girls' night.

The three of us gather around the fireplace in our pajamas and queue up some new reality TV show Julie's interested in. We're still chatting away when the doorbell rings.

"I got it!" Moxie jumps up to grab the door while I walk into the kitchen for some plates.

When I come back, Julie already has a slice of pizza hanging out of her mouth, and Moxie is laughing at something on the TV.

"I guess there's no need for plates." I shake my head and grab a slice. "What's this?"

There's black writing on top of the pizza box.

What do you do when life hands you lemons and no sugar?

I eye the ladies in front of me. "Is this for you guys?"

"Huh?" Julie turns to me and reads the box. "Oh, no. That's for you. What *do* you do when life hands you lemons and no sugar?"

"You cut the lemons and grab the whiskey, duh!" Moxie and I say together.

Back when we were kids, Amy had Bunco nights with a few of her friends. A whiskey sour was Amy's favorite drink to make—still is to this day. All the other women loved them too and raved about them to everyone they knew. I have no doubt that if my mom were still alive back then, she would have loved the drink and Amy too.

There's a small pang in my chest with the thought. I finish the slice of pizza in my hand and walk back into the kitchen to grab the whiskey.

As I open the liquor cabinet, a gold card wedged between two bottles catches my eye. I can't help but smile as I reach for it and tear it open.

I can't stop thinking about you while I'm away. These conferences would be much more interesting with your mouth wrapped around my cock. Be my perfect little slut and lift your skirt, slide your panties to one side, and take a picture for me.

Holy shit. He's a thousand miles away and still manages to make this hot. I jump as someone clears their throat behind me.

"Whatcha got there?" Moxie snatches it out of my hand. I make a grab for it, but she's too quick. She turns and runs back into the living room.

"Hey!" I call after her.

"Ewww! Is that from Tucker?" She tosses the card at me. "Keep that in the bedroom please! How am I going to look Amy in the eye now?"

Julie stares at us, laughing. "Let me see."

Moxie picks up the card before I can reach it and hands it to her.

Julie's face becomes a bright shade of red. "Whew! That's steamy." She fans herself with the card and hands it back to me.

"I don't see the problem here. You're the one who had sex on her couch," I point a finger at Moxie, then take the card from Julie.

Moxie laughs and rolls her eyes while Julie raises her hands in surrender. "She wasn't supposed to be home. Oops!"

We make our way back to the couch and finish the episode of the TV show before I excuse myself to the bathroom.

Moxie's teasing voice floats down the hallway. "Better make it sexy!"

Julie snorts. "Moxie!"

"Oh, cut it out," I call back to them. I roll my eyes, close the bathroom door, and prepare to take a picture to send my insatiable boyfriend, knowing his appetite will only increase when he sees it.

Chapter Twenty-Two

Tucker

Lizzy: Found the clue

Lizzy: (Incoming Picture)

Me: Mmm. Do you have any idea what I'm going to do to you when I get home?

Lizzy: I can only imagine, Sir.

Me: (Incoming Picture)

Me: It's extremely hard to concentrate on this last presentation when my mind is filled with all these dirty thoughts about you.

Lizzy: Downright lickable.

Me: Such a perfect little slut.

Lizzy: Yes, Sir. I love it when you call me your little slut. Makes me feel owned by you and loved by you.

Me: Gotta go! I love you.

Lizzy: I love you too, Sir.

This woman never ceases to amaze me. After I make my way back to my seat in the back row, I palm my cock under the table to relieve some of the ache, and stifle a groan. Thank god they have black tablecloths at this event. The last ones were sheer, and sheer is not a good look on anything.

I glance at the time on my phone. Almost time to call it a night. As much as I usually enjoy listening to inspirational talks on how to expand your brand and learning new ways to manage what you say to prospective clients, Lizzy is all I can think about.

Her breathy moans filling my ears. Her lips touching mine. Her hands wrapped around my cock.

When we moved into her house, I made it my personal mission to fuck her on every surface I could. And there's a shit ton of surfaces in, and around, that old house.

Lizzy deserves to be worshipped and loved with no conditions. She's got that fierce fire behind her eyes, taunts me with everything she has, and takes everything I give her and still offers up more.

She's my perfect kind of submissive. She's everything my heart desires.

A round of applause erupts in the conference room, and I follow suit to keep up the charade. I have no idea what this guy spent the last twenty minutes talking about. I'm gathering up my things when I spot Mike coming toward me.

Mike is one of the first colleagues I met years ago, during a conference similar to this one. He lives in Washington, although I keep trying to drag him to the Midwest with me. We could work phenomenally together—he'd just need to give up the coast.

"Yo, Tucker! It's been a while, man." He brings me in for a hug.

"Yeah, it's been a year?" I chuckle. We talk weekly, but it's been a year since our last conference together.

He looks me up and down. "Up for a drink? You look like you could use one."

Shaking my head, I answer, "Don't I know it. Where to?"

We head down to the hotel lobby and sit at the bar. I was hoping for somewhere outside of the hotel, but as soon as I sit down, I realize I'm too tired to go out anyway.

Mike signals the bartender. "Two whiskeys on the rocks, and make his a double." That earns a chuckle out of me.

"Better make his a double too," I call after her. She appears a moment later with two Old Fashioned glasses and sets them down in front of us.

"Put it on my tab, darling."

"You got it, Mike." She winks at him and dashes across the bar to help the next customer.

"Oooh, she knows you by name. Does she scream it in the bedroom too?" I snort and take a sip, trying to suppress the cough that follows the burn. "Ugh, I don't know why I let you get me whiskey. Lizzy does the same thing. I hate that stuff."

He balks. "Whatever, man. Let me tell you about this girl I'm seeing." He missed our last three calls because of this mystery woman.

I pick up my glass and swirl the liquid around the ice. I'm trying to pay attention to what Mike is saying, but my mind wanders back to Lizzy.

"Anyway, I think she might be the one." Not sure why that line pulls me back to our conversation. He's grinning and has a twinkle in his eye.

I blink a few times before responding. "Huh? Oh, that's great, Mike. I'm happy for you."

"Thanks, man. I'm very lucky. How's your mom and everyone?"

"They're good, always keeping busy. Moxie more so than everyone. She's knee-deep in the new restaurant. Rhett's pestering her about having a baby. Mom is trying to meddle in my life, but she's good."

"Well, you are the baby of the family, and you're the only boy," he points out.

He makes a valid point. While I am my mom's only biological child, she did take two others under her wing over the years. Moxie is one of them, and only a year older than I am. Jenny is the other, sitting at three years older than Moxie, and is the one with twin girls. Mom fawns over the twins, who like to keep her on her toes.

"And Elizabeth?"

"Ah, saving the best for last," I say playfully. "She's fantastic. Going through a bit of a rough patch between her father and a new situation at work, but she's strong and resilient." I pull my phone out of my pocket to show him a picture she recently took of us.

"Gorgeous, man. You look happy," he remarks.

"I am," I agree, shoving the phone back in my pocket. I down the last of my drink and slam the glass on the counter. "Okay, I have to call it a night. It's an early flight tomorrow. It was great seeing you, Mike."

"You too, Tucker." He stands up and shakes my hand. "I might fly out your way sometime."

I nod, knowing it's just something he says. It would take immense persuasion for him to move to Crimson. "You're welcome anytime. Thanks for the drink."

"Have a good night, and safe travels tomorrow."

We part ways at the elevator. I'm going up, and he's heading home. I take the elevator to the tenth floor, saunter to my room, and open the door. Before jumping into bed, I lay out my clothes for tomorrow and pack up the rest. Something white falls out of my dress pants pocket and lands on the floor.

I pick it up and finger the edges. It's a small envelope, like the kind you'd receive with flowers. *Where'd this come from?* I lift the flap and a familiar scent fills my nose. Pulling out the card, my heart swells with love as I read the words.

You are an exceptional man, Tucker. You bring out the best in me, and without you, I wouldn't know what true love can feel like. Come home to me. I'll be waiting. xoxo

Tomorrow can't come soon enough.

Chapter
Twenty-Three

Tucker

AFTER ENSURING THE TARP is secured for the third time, I hook my phone up to the small speakers on the table and queue up the playlist. There's only five minutes until Julie arrives with Lizzy.

Julie has blindfolded Lizzy, and she'll help her walk to me. I've asked for Julie's help numerous times in the past twenty-four hours since I've been home. She's been my lifesaver.

When I had to take Kristie's place at the conference in Washington at short notice because she came down with the flu, I was sure this would be a wreck. These things take time. Hours of brainstorming, days of planning for any and all contingencies, and, of course, all the prep work for the day of. But we managed to pull it all off, and everything came together in the end.

Tires crunch over the gravel, drawing my attention to the left. My heart thumps loudly in my chest, and I take a deep breath. Lizzy sits in the passenger seat, blindfolded, while Julie gets out of the car and runs around to open the door for her. Julie grabs Lizzy's hands and helps her out of the car, then carefully guides her toward me.

"We're almost there, just a few more steps." Julie smiles at me.

"Where are we?" Lizzy pauses. "Wait, I know those sounds. Why are we at the lake?"

She guides Lizzy to the chair sitting in front of me, facing the lake, and when Lizzy takes the blindfold off, she'll see me, with a backdrop of the stunning sunset over the water.

Lizzy moves her head side to side. "Julie?"

I put my finger to my lips and crouch down on one knee in front of Lizzy. Slowly, I take the blindfold off.

Her eyes crinkle in confusion. Light classical music starts in the background.

"Tucker?"

"Sunshine, I crave the most innocent parts of our relationship. Like sitting in front of the fire, holding hands, and watching a movie. Our good night kisses, and the way I can always tell you how much I adore you." Her eyes widen, but I continue. "When I look at you, I see the one I love, the one I need, the one I'm meant to be with. You are the strongest woman I've had the pleasure of knowing, and I am so lucky to be by your side."

Her hands fly up to her mouth, covering a gasp, as I open the ring box. "Marry me, Lizzy. Be my wife, and I promise you, no one will work harder to make you happy and cherish you more than me."

"Of course, yes!" She screams and flies out of the chair, knocking me over into the sand, and peppers me with kisses.

Julie shouts from the sidelines, "Aww, yay!"

We stand up as Julie walks toward us. I slide the ring on Lizzy's finger—a perfect fit. She flashes her finger at Julie, who gawks at the ring.

"Girl, that thing is gorgeous!" They laugh.

"Oh, Tucker." Lizzy wraps her arms around my neck and kisses me hungrily.

"And that's my cue to go. Congratulations, guys. Love you both!" She's about halfway to her car when I call out for her.

"Julie, thank you." She gives me a thumbs up before climbing back in her car and driving away.

Lizzy looks around in amazement. "What's all this?" She walks under the awning and runs her fingers down the length of the table.

Annie was able to pipe "she said yes" in frosting on my girl's favorite brownies. I laid them out in a curve and laid a bunch of daisies in front of them, surrounded by confetti-paper hearts.

She grabs one of the brownies and takes a big bite, leaving some frosting on the tip of her nose.

"You got something right—" I reach out and swipe the frosting off. "There." I turn my finger around to show her the frosting. She leans toward my finger, then closes her eyes and sucks the frosting off.

I groan. "Now, now. If you can't behave . . ." I leave the threat hanging.

A smirk crosses her face. "If I can't behave what, Sir?" Her fiery eyes meet mine, and I capture her lips in a bruising kiss. She drops the rest of the brownie on the table and wraps her arms around my neck.

I drop my hands to her waist and pull her closer.

"Here, now," she pants.

I walk us backward until the other table hits her hips, then I lift her up, making quick movements. "I can't wait until you're mine, the future Mrs. Tucker Banks."

"I'm already yours," she murmurs against my lips. I bunch her flowy skirt up around her hips, pull her panties to the side, and plunge into her, taking her breath away. Lizzy moans. "Oooh."

"Fuck, you're so tight, baby." She hooks her legs around the back of mine and pulls me deeper into her, and I groan. "You're mine," I say, then I bite her neck, claiming her.

"All yours," she pants as she writhes against me. "Fuck. Tucker, I need to come. Please, Sir."

"Not yet, baby." I capture her lips again and flick my tongue into her mouth. My hips buck against her. "Mmm, you feel so fucking good."

She whimpers, and I fuck her harder against the table. "Come for me, Sunshine."

Euphoria softens her features, and we come together. There's a moment of serene bliss between us.

Then her phone rings, followed by a series of dings.

"You'd better get that." I kiss down her neck, slowly pull out of her, and adjust my clothes.

She hops down off the table and fixes her clothes, then grabs her phone out of her purse.

"What the?" She turns the phone to me. *Six missed calls from Crimson Senior Living Center. 1 new Voicemail.*

I take it from her, dial her voicemail, and put it on speaker.

"Hello, this is a message for Elizabeth Carter. I'm calling from the Crimson Senior Living Center regarding your dad, Roger. Miss Carter, we've been trying to contact you urgently. Due to his declining condition, he has fallen into a coma. We don't believe he has long. Please come at your earliest convenience. Thank you."

Her face falls, and she takes a staggering step back. *This bastard has taken everything from her. I won't let him ruin this too.*

"Lizzy. Lizzy." I squeeze her hand. "Come back to me."

She blinks a few times, shakes her head, then stares blankly at the darkening sky. It's twilight now, the last little bit of the sun's rays disappearing behind the horizon. "I just need a minute," she whispers.

I guide her to the chair and kiss her forehead before shutting off the music. Then I start packing everything up, stealing glances at her every other second. She's just sitting there, frail, while she tries to process what's happening.

Every fiber of my being hates the effect he has on her. From all the physical abuse she endured as a child to the greedy manipulation as an adult, she doesn't deserve any of this. Not one bit.

After everything is placed in the trunk of my car, I run back to Lizzy and secure her in my arms. I carry her back to the car and buckle her up.

"Let's get you home, Sunshine."

Epilogue

TEN MONTHS LATER . . .

There's a quiet knock on the door.

"Yes, it's open!" I twist my arm behind me and tuck something into the ribbon that spans my waist.

Music drifts in as Amy peeks her head inside before fully entering the room. "You almost ready, dear?"

I meet her gaze through the reflection in the mirror. "Almost. Would you mind helping me with this clasp?"

"Of course." She advances through the room and takes either side of the necklace in her hands. I bend down a little so she can wrap it around my neck, and she clips the clasp in place. "There you go. It's beautiful."

My fingers trace the necklace down to the topaz stone woven into the metal. "Yes, it is. It was my mom's—my something old."

"And you have your something new, borrowed, and blue?" Her eyes light up.

"Yes, ma'am, I do." I hold out my wrist to show her the something borrowed. It's a thin, gold bangle from Moxie. My something blue is the garter on my leg . . . it's my new bra and underwear too, but my future mother-in-law doesn't need to know that.

She kisses my cheek then flips the thin veil over my face. "You look stunning, Lizzy. Like you've stepped right out of a magazine. Your mom would be so proud." She squeezes my shoulders. "But no crying, we can't mess up the face that took hours!"

I laugh and run my hands down the front of my dress. It's a stunning V-neck with an A-line ruffle skirt, light on the ruffles. Truly, though, I do feel like crying. It's my big day, and the person I miss the most isn't here to witness me getting married. I carry her with me in my heart, and I know she's smiling, looking down on me. Taking a deep breath, I start walking toward the door.

"Oh, hold on, dear. I almost forgot!" Amy pulls a small baggie out of her purse with a roll of tape. "We can't forget this. Here, let me see your foot."

Bunching up my dress, I stick out my foot. She shows me the item in her hand. It's a penny from the year Tucker and I met. Then she tapes it on the inside of the heel, underneath the sole.

"Thank you, Amy. For everything."

"Hush, now. It's Mom, if that's okay with you."

I sniffle and nod my head. "Thank you, Mom." I wrap my arms around her, bringing her into a hug. She's always felt like family, but she was always Amy in the back of my mind.

Today, everything changes.

"Here Comes the Bride" floats through the door.

"It's time. Are you ready?"

"Let's get married!" I exclaim. I'm certainly nervous as I take the exquisite bouquet from Amy and hook my arm through hers.

As we walk down the hallway to the ballroom, the moment I asked Amy to walk with me flashes through my mind.

The night I got the call about my father, Tucker took me straight home. I couldn't face my emotions. It's like he read my mind. He never once asked if I wanted to go see Roger. He didn't assume I wanted to either.

We arrived home that night, and I crawled into bed and fell into a deep sleep. I vaguely remember Tucker dressing me in pajamas and tucking me in. Everything was heavy.

But when I woke up the next morning, I felt a sense of relief. I couldn't explain it. I felt lighter than I had in years. I rolled over in bed and picked up my phone. We hadn't told anyone yet, outside of Julie. The only other person I wanted to tell was Amy.

I knew I should have let Tucker tell her, but I needed to talk to her. I couldn't help myself, which is why the first thing I said to her was, "Walk me down the aisle?"

After a moment of shrieking, she accepted. She knew the proposal was coming because, as it turns out, the ring Tucker gave me was his grandmother's. It was at that moment Tucker walked in with breakfast. The look on his face was pure excitement. He took the phone from me, silently commanded me to eat, and started talking to his mom.

That look was one thing, but the look on his face now, as I round the corner and start walking down the aisle . . . that's something I'll never forget.

It's one of those moments where the groom gasps and is completely in awe. Standing next to him is Rhett as the best man and Mike as his groomsman. Opposite them is Julie as the maid of honor, and Moxie as my bridesmaid, who was chatting up Mike about Julie as they walked down the aisle. Isn't it customary for the maid of honor to hook up with a groomsman?

The room is decorated with daisies surrounded by pink carnations. Twinkle lights illuminate the aisle and are woven between the chairs in each row. Our altar is an archway lined with pale pink drapes.

With each step I take down the aisle toward the man who will be my husband, my soul feels more at home. I'm recharged surrounded by the people who love me and accept me for who I am. Everything in my life is a reflection of a choice I've made, and this is the best one yet.

Tucker reaches for me as I take the last step to the altar. Amy guides my hand into his and kisses my cheek again. I turn and face Tucker as we start our new chapter together. The officiant begins.

"First, a verse about love: 1 Corinthians 13:4-7. Love is patient . . ." I zone out, seeing nothing but Tucker as the officiant reads the rest of the verse. He squeezes my hand in reassurance.

"And now, the rings. The bride and groom opted to write their vows. Tucker?"

Tucker takes my left hand and gazes into my eyes. "Lizzy. I wanted to shut you up. That's why our first kiss happened." He pauses, and I hear snickers coming from the crowd. "The thought of kissing you stuck in my mind for years to come. When we kissed for the second time, I knew I'd never let you go. Now that I have you, I will continue to choose you over and over again, in a heartbeat. It's always been you, and I vow to spend the rest of my life appreciating you, loving you at your weakest moments and at your greatest. Marriage is not easy, and it can get ugly, but it can also be the most amazing thing in the world. It's full of difficult days, but it's my promise to you to make the continued decision to love you even when it's hard, because I'm aware no one is perfect, but you are so worth it." Tucker slides the ring on my finger.

"Elizabeth?" The officiant turns to me.

"Tucker, you've opened my eyes to things I never knew were possible. With you by my side, I know I can fearlessly take on the world. This is my vow to you: I promise to love you completely each day, to build our dreams together, and to work through any obstacle in our way. My love for you is unconditional, and it will never be anything but. We're a team; you never have to do anything alone. You've shown me how true love does exist, and I'm a better person because of you. My heart was made to love you, to cherish you, and to stay by your side on the most difficult days." I slide the ring on his finger.

"Now, the fun part. Tucker, will you lift Elizabeth's veil?"

Tucker lets go of my hands to lift my veil.

"One more thing." I lean back on my heels and reach behind my back. I shove the test into his hands and grip them both with mine. "My best friend, the love of my life—you're going to be a dad."

I don't think I've ever seen Tucker smile so big. He comes forward and pulls me into a kiss, his lips crushing mine.

Cheers fill the room as the officiant says loudly, "I now present to you Mr. and Mrs. Banks, and baby."

"Get a room!" someone yells from the audience.

"They already did!" someone else yells over the cheers from our friends and family.

I giggle against Tucker's mouth and crinkle my nose. We break apart and face the audience as Mendelssohn's "Wedding March" begins to play.

Hand in hand, we jump off the small stage and run down the aisle toward the limo waiting to whisk us into the sunset.

However, Tucker has a different idea. He pulls us into the closest bathroom and locks the door behind us.

I see the fire burning in his eyes, and I yearn to play with it.

The End

Lucy: Ricky, we're revolting.
Ricky: No more than usual.

I Love Lucy - Season 1 Episode 25

Countdown Madness Playlist

Bring On The Rain by Jo De Messina
The Thunder Rolls by State Of Mine
Red Flags by Spencer Crandall
So Much for My Happy Ending by Avril Lavigne
Singles You Up by Jordan Davis
Paris in the Rain by Lauv
Let Me Be Sad by I Prevail
Impossible by Nothing But Thieves
Time After Time by Cyndi Lauper
Grind With Me by Pretty Ricky
Just the Way by Parmalee
I'm Yours by Jason Mraz
Shackles by Steven Rodriguez
I'm Gonna Getcha Good by Shania Twain
Gimme That Girl by Joe Nichols
Love You Like The Movies by Anthem Lights
Dressed Up in White by CAL

Lizzy and Tucker's Recipes

Double-Fudge Brownies

Ingredients:

<u>Brownies</u>

1 box (18.2 ounces) Duncan Hines Dark Chocolate Fudge Brownie mix

1 large egg

⅓ cup of water

½ cup of avocado oil* (or vegetable oil)

<u>Ganache</u>

1 cup of heavy whipping cream (or heavy cream)

8 ounces of quality semi-sweet chocolate**, finely chopped

Instructions:

Make the brownies according to the box.

Let brownies cool for about an hour or until they are not warm to the touch.

While the brownies bake, add semi-sweet chocolate to a mixing bowl.

Heat the cream in a small saucepan over medium heat until it begins to slightly simmer. Do not let it come to a boil. Then remove from heat and let it sit for two minutes.

Slowly pour the cream over the chocolate and mix until combined.

Let the ganache sit at room temperature to cool and thicken.

Once the brownies and ganache have cooled, frost the brownies.

Enjoy with your favorite ice cream on top or with your favorite cup of coffee.

Notes:

* Avocado oil is a personal preference, but the recipe can be used with either vegetable, canola, or avocado oil. The recipe has not been tried with coconut oil.

** The semi-sweet chocolate should be in baking bars, not chocolate chips. Chocolate chips can be used as a last resort, but they may be harder to melt and can result in the ganache not being as smooth.

Whiskey Sour

Ingredients:

2 ounces (4 tablespoons) of your favorite whiskey

1 ounce (2 tablespoons) of fresh lemon juice

¾ ounce (1 ½ tablespoons) of simple syrup (or pure maple syrup)

Garnish with an orange peel and/or a cocktail cherry

Ice, for serving

Instructions:

Add the whiskey, lemon juice, and syrup into a cocktail shaker.

Fill the shaker with ice and shake until the drink is cold.

Strain the drink into an Old Fashioned glass. Serve with ice, and garnish to your liking.

He Calls Me Bug

by Zoey Zane
Sneak Peek

Thanks for reading Countdown Madness! Did you enjoy Tucker and Lizzy's story? Please consider leaving a review on Amazon and Goodreads! Continue reading for a sneak peek of He Calls Me Bug, re-releasing with bonus content, on 20th September 2022.

Pre-order available on Amazon!

He Calls Me Bug is a taboo novella between two consenting people who are of age. There are instances of abuse (physical, psychological, and sexual) and cheating, none of which are between the two main characters. If any of these triggers make you uncomfortable, this may not be the book for you.

Prologue

I HAVE ALWAYS HEARD the heart wants what it wants, and there is no use in fighting it. My dad is the first one I heard that from, and I've heard it many times over again throughout the years. That's why he married my mom. There was no one else for him. There never would be.

I could see the kind of life they have, and I knew that was the kind of love I wanted; the kind of love I *needed*. But, as I started to grow up, I learned not everyone thought of love that way. Not everyone had the love my parents have, nor did they believe it would happen for them. My Uncle Davey was proof of this—he was someone who wanted to be loved, but only found love with all the wrong people.

Chapter One

Sky

NINE YEARS OLD . . .

Not many people leave a lasting impression on a nine-year-old. The first time I see Uncle Davey, he is sitting on my favorite couch, in my favorite spot, holding a beer in his hand. I walk into the living room, stop in my tracks, and drop my backpack.

"Who are you?"

"Sky, mind your manners." My daddy walks into the living room with his beer. "Pick up your backpack and come meet my friend."

Without taking my eyes off this man—this stranger—I grab my backpack and hang it up. I slowly back up toward my daddy when the man chuckles.

"It's okay, James." He turns to look at me. "Hi. I'm your Uncle Davey."

"I don't have an Uncle Davey." I continue to stare him down.

Uncle Davey smiles and puts his hands up in surrender.

"Remember the guy I used to work with back in San Diego? This is David Sullivan, my best friend," my daddy says.

"But my friends call me Davey. We can be friends, can't we, Bug?" Uncle Davey holds out his hand.

I take a few steps toward him and hesitate. *Bug?* "Sure, as long as you get out of my spot." I place my hand in his, and we shake. His firm grip sends tingles down my spine as he gives my hand a gentle squeeze.

He lets out a thundering laugh and stands up. "I think this is the beginning of a beautiful friendship."

The rest of the night goes on, and I cling to Uncle Davey's side. He makes funny voices and yells at the

TV when the ball goes the wrong way. By bedtime, my stomach hurts from how hard I've laughed.

"Good night, Uncle Davey. I hope you come back." I give a slight wave to Uncle Davey, hug my daddy, and head up the stairs.

Uncle Davey nods. "You bet. Good night, Bug." My heart squeezes when he calls me that. I think I like being called Bug.

I wake up a short time later to get some water. It's one of the warmer nights we've had in a while. I walk into the bathroom and fill up my cup, but as I walk back to my room, I hear voices downstairs. Stepping over the top step to avoid any squeaks, I walk down a few steps. I stop before the landing, hidden by the wall, and settle in to listen.

"She's just so infuriating!" a voice booms from below.

"What's the problem this time?" My dad always tries to fix problems that aren't his.

"She treats me like shit, James. Kristie would have a fit if she knew I was talking to you about this."

My ears perk up. Who is Kristie?

"Kristie treats everyone like shit—has for as long as I've known her."

Uncle Davey sighs. "I know but she's my wife, man. I have to share my location with her, so she knows I'm not out doing god-knows-what with god-knows-who. If I even stop at a gas station outside of this damn radius, I'm in the doghouse. Aside from all the negativity she emits, I love her. But, unfortunately, the leash is short, and I don't know how much more of this I can take."

"At least she doesn't use the literal leash on you and make you walk around on all fours." My daddy snickers.

"And the sex is disappointing. Even when it happens, it's not worth it. But fuck, why couldn't she have a hell of a pussy? One that I'd love to keep fucking, despite all the shit. That'd be a reason to stay."

I gasp. Uncle Davey said bad words.

"So you'll put up with her a little more until you can't."

"I just wish she would love me the way I love her—unconditional, willing to go the extra mile to put a smile on my face, or just wrapping her arms around me for a warm hug. A phone call or a text when she's running late, maybe pick up my favorite beer on the way home from work, or just plan a date night for us. Damn, give me a *little* something to show you care."

The garage door closes, and I freeze. Then, I hear heels click across the kitchen and realize my mommy is home. I slide down another step so I can peer around the corner.

"David? Oh my god, it's been a while! How are you? James didn't tell me you were stopping by." My mom reaches to hug Uncle Davey.

"Jessica, good to see you."

Jessica kisses my daddy on the forehead. "Don't stay up too late. I'm going to take a bath and lie down." She winks at Daddy and saunters off to their bedroom.

"See, you need to get a woman who says she's taking a bath when she really means 'I'll be waiting for you.' And that woman is not Kristie," my daddy says and takes a sip of his beer.

"I've never understood how you found her, but you have a good woman. Kristie is nothing compared to Jessica."

"Hey, now! Hands and eyes off my woman." Daddy laughs. "You can have that kind of love too, you know. It's not about being possessive, bitchy, and high-maintenance. It's about the mutual respect you have for each other, admiration, and the understanding that the two of you are in this for the long haul. Sadly, Kristie doesn't have those traits, and unfortunately, I don't think she ever will."

I hear my daddy say goodbye a few moments later, and the front door closes. I run up the stairs and jump back into bed before someone catches me.

All at once, and in a matter of seconds, I realize three things. One: Uncle Davey needs to be loved fiercely but gently. Two: Kristie, whoever she is, is not the one for him. And three: there will never be anyone else for me. Uncle Davey is mine.

Chapter Two

David

I PULL INTO THE driveway, dreading going inside. Kristie knew I would be visiting James for the evening, but I didn't expect to be gone for so long.

A light flickers upstairs, and a figure appears in the window.

Uh oh. This is not good.

I turn off the car and walk up to the front door. I turn the lock, walk into the kitchen, and set my keys on the table. Opening the fridge, I grab a water bottle and head upstairs to face my punishment.

She's waiting for me when I open our bedroom door, and she doesn't look happy.

"You're lucky I checked your location and you were still at James's."

"Kristie, it's been a long night. Can we please not do this?" I pull my shirt over my head and take off my pants.

"No. You're late."

I sigh and head to the bathroom. Kristie steps in front of me. "Excuse me," I say.

She doesn't move, just keeps holding her stance.

"What are you doing? I need to piss."

Her eyes darken, and she doesn't blink.

"Come on, Kristie. I need to piss. We can deal with this tomorrow. It's late."

"You can hold it. Fifteen minutes."

I try to sidestep her and she slaps me right across the face.

"I said, you can hold it." She looks at her watch.

The seconds slowly tick by: tick-tock, tick-tock. I would have hit her back if this had been another time, another place, another life. But instead, I wait.

This shit hurts.

As soon as the fifteen minutes are up, she steps to the side, and I rush into the bathroom. I slam the door and do my business. I'm brushing my teeth when I hear a knock on the door. "Go away, Kristie."

"I'm not done with you yet."

Fuck, not tonight. "Not tonight."

"Yes, tonight. I've been waiting for you all night. So get out here, big boy, and come claim your prize."

She opens the door and drapes her arm on the door frame, trying to nail the seductive pose she's never able to get quite right. I look up at her before spitting out the toothpaste and rinsing my mouth. She steps toward me and reaches for my cock, runs her fingers over my length.

Sighing, I walk toward the bedroom, walking Kristie backward until her knees hit the bed. I lean in to kiss her and lay her down. Instead, she puts her hands on my chest and pushes me off her. She points to the bed in a silent command for me to lay down.

I obey her, and she peppers my chest with kisses, working her way down my stomach. God, I wish she'd keep going, but she stops short at the top of my boxers. I nudge her head down, and she glares at me. At least I tried.

"Not tonight, big boy."

Not any night.

She pulls my boxers down to reveal my erection.

"My, my. Someone is excited."

She straddles me, reaches between her legs, and spreads some of her wetness onto my hard cock. Then, she teases my hardened tip against her slit.

"Kristie . . ."

Slowly, she lowers herself onto my cock, and I groan. Kristie starts rocking back and forth and leans forward, shoving her tits in my face. I reach up and squeeze one, twisting the nipple just the way she likes. In no time, she's almost at her climax, and I'm nowhere near close.

In an effort to make it feel good, I sit up and grab the back of her head with my hand. I grip her hair, lean her back, and breathe, "Fuck." Her breaths falter, and she moans.

I'm almost there. Maybe she'll let me finish this time, but before I can come, she climaxes.

"Sorry, big boy. The only way you're coming tonight is in that bathroom." She climbs off me and slides underneath the covers.

"Come on, Kristie. Help me out."

"You've been a bad boy, and bad boys don't get help to come."

What a bitch. I take a deep breath, get off the bed, and grab a clean pair of boxers from the dresser. Kristie's done with me for the night.

Unfortunately, my cock didn't get the message my brain was sending. I head into the bathroom and turn on the shower like Kristie demands. I pull out my phone and navigate to my favorite porn site. Her juices still coat my cock, but I pull out the bottle of lube anyway. After I prop up my phone against the sink, I start rubbing my hand up and down, wishing Kristie would let me do all the dirty things I crave. All the dirty things she never allows me to do. Wishing I could shove my cock down her throat and make her choke. Wishing I could penetrate my cock in her wet pussy while I fuck her from behind. Then, just as I imagine sliding in and out of her, I come, stifling my groan with a towel.

After rinsing off in the shower, I dry off and pull on my boxers. I open the door, and Kristie is nowhere to be seen. All I see is my pillow on top of the blanket—the key indicator I'm to sleep on the couch tonight.

I set up my make-shift bed on the couch and turn on the TV. A replay of tonight's game is on. I just want some noise in this otherwise quiet house. The hall light turns off behind me, and I hear the soft click of the bedroom door closing. No *good night*, no *I love you*, not a peep from her.

As I try to ponder where our marriage went wrong, something James said rings in my head. *"You can have that kind of love too, you know."* Those are the last words I think of before I fall asleep.

More from Zoey Zane:

A Beautiful Broken Life

Coming Soon:

He Calls Me Bug – re-releasing with bonus content
09.20.2022
(previously in the Cheaters Anthology)
Sweet Like Sugar, Thick Like Honey
Naughty Doctor

Meet Zoey

Zoey Zane is an author and poet, but will always be a zealous reader at heart. She has a love for dark romance and thrillers, the two genres that dominate most of the space on her bookshelves. Zoey lives in Tennessee with her husband, their son, and their two adorable pit bulls.

You can find me at zoeyzane.net, by scanning the QR code, or on the sites listed below!

𝕒 https://www.amazon.com/Zoey-Zane/e/B08K56BJZ2/

f https://www.facebook.com/zoeyzaneauthor

BB https://www.bookbub.com/authors/zoey-zane

𝑔 https://www.goodreads.com/author/show/20671544.Zoey_Zane

https://www.instagram.com/justmekendra/

Acknowledgments

Honey Bunches - I know it can be difficult to listen to my ramblings all the time. #SorryNotSorry. Thank you for the endless supply of Reese's pieces, orange slices, and most of all, your patience. Our adventure has barely begun.

Gwen - Ever my lifesaver. Thank you for helping me get the word out and for keeping me active.

Rachelle - Thank you for turning my story into a book. From editing to formatting, your input is so appreciated, and I love what you've done with it.

Pam - You're still with me, even though you're not. There have been countless times during the writing process where I knew you'd love it. My only hope is that you're dancing with your mom and that y'all are having the best time.

Made in the USA
Columbia, SC
27 July 2024

39454609R00162